CW01457772

DEFENSE
OF OTHERS

David Brunelle Legal Thriller #15

STEPHEN PENNER

ISBN: 9798218090999

Defense of Others

©2022 Stephen Penner. All rights reserved. No part of this book may be reproduced or transferred without the express written consent of the author.

This is a work of fiction. Any similarity with real persons or events is purely coincidental. Persons, events, and locations are either the product of the author's imagination or used fictitiously.

Joy Lorton, Editor.
Cover design by Nathan Wampler Book Covers.

DEFENSE
OF OTHERS

The use, attempt, or offer to use force upon or toward the person of another is not unlawful in the following cases:

...

Whenever used by a party about to be injured, or by another lawfully aiding him or her, in preventing or attempting to prevent an offense against his or her person

Revised Code of Washington 9A.16.020
Use of Force – When Lawful

CHAPTER 1

Just when you think you know someone, they go and get themselves murdered.

David Brunelle, homicide prosecutor with the King County Prosecutor's Office, pulled his aging sedan up to the crime scene that was wrapping itself around the brownstone office building in Seattle's Pioneer Square District, just down the hill from the courthouse. Most of the tenants there were solo attorneys, the kind who cobbled rent together from a combination of bankruptcies, divorces, and simple wills. And criminal defense. Always criminal defense. Microsoft or Amazon weren't going to hire you unless you had an undergraduate degree in a hard science and law degree from a top ten law school, but any schmuck with a bar card was allowed to represent a criminal defendant.

Only a few of those schmucks were good enough to make it big doing just criminal work, but the ones who did hosted clients and opponents in their penthouse suite with the view of Elliott Bay. Brunelle had been in that penthouse before, but never at one in the morning and never because it was his night to be the on-call homicide prosecutor. The last time he'd been to that building was on a Friday afternoon to begin his weekend by telling an overly confident and narcissistic defense attorney to pound sand and get ready for trial. That night, as he parked his car in the middle of the blocked-off street, nodded to the officer guarding the building's entrance, and tapped his foot during the caged elevator ride to the top floor, he discovered he'd come to see the same attorney.

"William Harrison Welles," Brunelle identified the bullet-riddled body, lying face up in front of his ostentatiously large oak desk, dead eyed, with a pool of blood soaked into the oriental rug under him. The I.D. was hardly necessary. After a long career of defending the accused in some of the city's most high-profile cases, the cops all knew William Harrison Welles. Especially the detectives whose own careers had overlapped Welles's.

"You are correct, sir," Larry Chen, homicide detective with the Seattle Police Department confirmed. They were standing on opposite sides of the body, both staring down at the victim in their next case. "Somehow, I'm not surprised he met his end this way. These defense attorneys live strange lives."

Brunelle nodded. Not all of them, of course. The only thing that was always true about generalizations was that they weren't always true. But Chen was right: a lot of the defense bar lived hard lives on the edge. He'd heard the stories of getting paid in drugs and sexual favors, of holding the murder weapon 'for safekeeping' in a desk drawer, of somehow even worse things. Welles had featured in a lot of those stories.

To be sure, there were plenty of defense attorneys Brunelle would have been surprised to be standing over at a 1:00 a.m. murder call-out. With Welles, Brunelle was only surprised it had taken so long.

"Any suspects?" Brunelle asked. He was going to need a defendant to charge.

"Everyone he's ever represented?" Chen ventured. "I'm guessing at least two ex-wives, maybe three? I mean, half my team here would have a motive for the way he treated them on some case or another over the years, but I think I can eliminate them."

Brunelle shrugged and grinned slightly. "Don't be too sure. Cops make the best murderers. No one suspects them."

Chen frowned. He seemed to take a moment to decide whether to engage Brunelle on that new topic of conversation, or stick with the possible suspects.

"We'll pull the security footage and see who entered the building seven hours after the end of the business day." Chen opted for the former topic. "I doubt whoever did this was here all night and then things just went bad all of a sudden."

Brunelle turned to scan the room. Murderers rarely cleaned up after the deed, especially not when the deed was accomplished with a firearm. Guns were loud. It raised the likelihood of detection, which raised the level of panic. A preplanned poisoning would probably leave a killer calm and collected enough to clean up the tea cups and wipe down the table. But a shooter who unloaded at least four shots, by Brunelle's initial glance at the body, would probably be thinking of only one thing: escape. Before the night custodian or another late-working tenant ran in to see what had happened. But the only glass sitting out was a nearly finished snifter of brandy on Welles's desk. There were no half-eaten boxes of take-out or a half-played hand of cards on the coffee table between the chairs by the windows. Whoever had done this had not been a guest of Welles's for the evening. Welles had been alone, until he wasn't.

And then he was dead.

Brunelle nodded. "You're right." That was the thing about evidence, circumstantial evidence, anyway. A thing happened, like a murder, and other things were left behind to tell the story like a turned over table, or not; a broken glass, or not; a bloody knife, or not. The room where it happened, so to speak, held the most evidence. But there was another location, of a sort, with just as vital information. Brunelle just needed to wait for it to be properly documented and separated from that room where it happened.

"You take care of this place, Larry," Brunelle gestured at the forensics officers already documenting the crime scene. "Come morning, I'll go to the autopsy."

CHAPTER 2

Brunelle stuck around Welles's office for a while, but the advantage of observing the autopsy versus observing the crime scene was that he could go home and grab a couple of hours of sleep before the autopsy. He could leave Chen to supervise the crime scene and feel like they were sharing the tasks even as his head hit the pillow. It might be for only a few hours, but it was a few hours more than Chen would get.

Autopsies weren't performed at crime scenes at 2:00 a.m. They were performed at the Medical Examiner's Office at 8:00 a.m., or later. The pathologists who carved open bodies to determine cause of death preferred to do that sort of thing in an actual examining room with actual equipment and proper lighting. So, unlike Brunelle and Chen, whichever assistant medical examiner would actually be making the 'Y' incision in Welles's torso got to sleep through the night, while technicians from the M.E.'s Office would be called out to the scene to collect the body, after the cops were done documenting everything.

Then the techs would wrap the hands in paper to preserve any trace evidence that might be trapped there, like the assailant's hair in clenched fists or even DNA under the fingernails. They would carefully transfer the body onto a sheet, then into a body bag, again to try to capture any trace evidence that might be on the victim's clothes or person. Then they would transport the body to the M.E.'s Office and put it into the freezer until the pathologist arrived at 8:00 a.m. Or 8:24 a.m., with a venti to-go cup.

Brunelle had arrived at 7:59, eager to observe the autopsy and glean any information regarding the details of how Welles met his end. The pathologist arrived at 8:24, that venti to-go cup in his hand and no particular urgency in his step or expression. He was a 30-something African American man, with a neatly trimmed beard and wire-rimmed glasses. He took a look at Brunelle, waiting humorlessly in the small lobby, but rather than address him directly, he walked up to the receptionist with a huge grin on his face and jerked a thumb at their guest.

"Who's the stiff?" He couldn't stop himself from laughing at his own joke, even as he finished it. Brunelle groaned.

"Sorry, sorry." The doctor hurried over to Brunelle and slapped a hand on his chest. "I couldn't help myself. I love making that joke."

"You make it a lot?" Brunelle wondered.

"Oh my God, yes," he answered. "Every chance I get. Which is more often than you might think."

Brunelle glanced over to the receptionist who confirmed the frequency of the joke with a pained nod of her head.

"Mike Donovan," the doctor introduced himself. "You're either a detective or a lawyer. And I'm guessing lawyer. Probably a prosecutor, right?"

Brunelle nodded. He didn't ask how Donovan knew, but Donovan told him anyway.

"You guys are the only ones wearing suits anymore," Donovan explained, "and the only ones who would show up at eight in the morning for an autopsy. Your suit is nice, though, so you're probably not a cop. You also look exhausted, so I'm guessing you were out at the murder scene in the middle of the night, and that means you're a prosecutor, not a defense attorney. Can't have those pesky defense attorneys at a crime scene messing everything up."

"There was a defense attorney at the crime scene," Brunelle informed him.

"There was?" Donovan seemed genuinely surprised, although he tempered his expression with a drag from his coffee cup.

"Yeah," Brunelle confirmed, "and now he's in your freezer."

Donovan's eyes widened. "Did you kill him?"

Brunelle's eyes followed suit. "What? No. Of course not."

Donovan exhaled audibly. "Oh, thank goodness. Otherwise this was going to be really awkward. You'd be backseat autopsying the whole time. 'There were three gunshots.' 'Four, but I missed one.'" He mocked their exchange. "I do not need that kind of pressure."

Brunelle wasn't sure what to say. A rare feeling for a lawyer.

Donovan patted him on the chest again. "Come on, Mr. Prosecutor. Let's go see what killed your friend."

"He wasn't a friend," Brunelle insisted.

But Donovan smiled sideways at him. "I don't interpret just dead bodies, sir. And you are not good at hiding your thoughts."

Brunelle actually felt like he was good at that, but Donovan waited a moment, then added. "No, you're not. Now come on."

Brunelle had to take a moment before reaching out to grab the door to the interior of the M.E.'s Office before it closed behind Donovan. He hurried after the good doctor and soon found himself outside the main examining room, and the entrance to the connected observation room next door.

"What's the name of your friend?" Donovan asked. "I'm guessing I've got a few of them piled up in the freezer. We can do him first."

"He's not my—" Brunelle started to protest again, before thinking better of it. "Welles. William Harrison Welles."

"Ooh," Donovan admired. "I like that name. No wonder he's your friend."

Brunelle dropped his head to the side at Donovan, then realized he was being teased. At 8:30 in the morning. At an autopsy. "Can we just get on with it?"

Donovan frowned slightly, but in a way that still seemed like a smile. "Fine. Strictly business. I get it." He nodded at the door to the observation room. "You gonna watch from in there?"

Brunelle considered for a moment. "No. I think I'd like to observe more closely than that. " He waited a beat. "Since he was a friend and all."

Donovan grinned at that, but didn't reply directly to it. Instead, he nodded toward the examining room. "I'll have the body brought in and meet you in there in a few minutes. I just need to pull on my protective gear."

Brunelle frowned. "It's not like you need to worry about risk of infection," he pointed out.

"Oh, it's not for them," Donovan explained. "It's for me. It can get pretty gross sometimes. Weird liquids shooting out unexpectedly."

He and Brunelle both took a moment to look at Brunelle's suit, nicer than what a detective would wear.

"You'll be fine though," Donovan assured him, before quickly disappearing down the hallway to conceal his laughter.

Brunelle shoved his hands in his pockets. He felt fairly confident they had extra protective gear they could have offered him. Then again, he didn't really expect much fluid to be squirting out of Welles's body. Most of his blood had drained out onto his office floor. What little was left was probably half frozen after a few hours in the freezer. But he might stand a step or two behind Donovan in any event.

A few minutes later, two technicians rolled Welles's body into the room, still inside a closed body bag, and transferred it, bag and all, onto one of the three metal examining tables in the room. A few minutes after that, Donovan returned, having only pulled an unbuttoned white lab coat over his clothes. He was still carrying his coffee.

Brunelle pointed at the obvious lack of truly protective gear.

Donovan shrugged. "I was just messing with you. Really, I needed to go to the little medical examiner's room. Nothing's going to squirt out on us. He's been dead for hours. Whatever fluid is left in his body has already pooled at the bottom. It's like trying to get water out of one of those coolers but it's almost empty and the fluid level is below the nozzle."

Brunelle nodded, but didn't feel the need to reply audibly.

Donovan seemed to want a response, though. "You know? And then you have to tip the cooler forward just to get the last bit out? It's like that."

"Don't tip the body," Brunelle deduced. "Got it."

"Well, I'm probably going to have to tip the body," Donovan put a hand on his hip, "so I can see what's on the other side. But just watch your shoes, I guess."

Again, they both looked at Brunelle's shoes. They were not nicer than what a detective would wear. Brunelle was on his feet a lot. He opted for comfort over style.

"Or don't worry about it," Donovan amended.

"Can we just get on with this?" Brunelle rolled a hand at the doctor. It was already after 9:00 a.m. They should have been done by then. He hoped Chen was having a more productive time trying to locate the killer.

Donovan raised an apologetic hand. "Of course, of course. I'm sure this is difficult enough for you. You don't need me commenting on your choice in footwear." He reached out and grabbed ahold of the zipper on the body bag. "Let's get this party started."

Brunelle had found Donovan's repeated references to his alleged friendship with Welles annoying, but when the body bag opened and Brunelle could see the pale, lifeless face of someone he had known, for better and worse, for the better part of two decades, he couldn't deny feeling something more than he had at any of the other autopsies he'd observed, and not just because of the proximity.

Every other time Brunelle could think of, when he met a dead person, it was for the first time. He hadn't known them in life. So, while he possessed the same imagination as anyone else and could have, had he been so inclined, conjured up images of the dead person doing something an alive person would do: playing the piano, walking the dog, sipping a latte. Usually though, to the extent Brunelle did try to imagine anything like that, it was just a replay of the victim's last moments alive. Imagining them raising their hands in a vain attempt to protect themselves from the coming onslaught that would soon enough lead them to the same examining room Brunelle and Donovan were standing in just then. Brunelle just imagined what probably happened then plastered the victim's face onto a stock image of the crime.

Welles was different. Brunelle had seen that face dozens of times, maybe even hundreds. He didn't have any trouble imagining it doing something in life. Indeed, it was just the opposite. He had trouble believing Welles wasn't about to open his eyes, sit up and start arguing for a bail reduction or a dismissal for egregious and irremediable government misconduct. Brunelle unconsciously took a step backward, as if to give the corpse space should it choose to stand to deliver its closing argument.

"It's different when you know them, isn't it?" Donovan knew.

Brunelle could only nod. "Apparently." He squinted a bit at his erstwhile, but late, foe. "He's dead, right? Even with the blood drained out of his face, I expect his eyes to open."

Donovan stepped forward and stuck a gloved finger in a bullet wound directly over Welles's heart. "Oh yeah, he's dead."

Brunelle frowned slightly. It wasn't like they were going to get fingerprints from the gunshot wound, but Donovan's cavalier attitude was wearing thin. "Maybe you should be more careful, doctor."

Donovan looked down at his finger, still inside Welles's chest, then pulled it out with a squelching pop. "Probably, but it's not like this autopsy is going to be difficult. I'm pretty sure I know what killed him."

"Multiple gunshot wounds," Brunelle knew that already. What he was interested in was something he couldn't see at 2:00 a.m. when the body was covered in clothes and blood and half-lit by the reading lamp on Welles's desk. He needed the body stripped, the lights overhead. "Anterior or posterior?" he asked.

Donovan stuck out an impressed lip. "Nice use of pathologist jargon, counselor," he admired. "Let me check."

Donovan examined the four holes in Welles's chest, then went to roll Welles's body onto its side to look at the back. "Can you help me out, Mr. Brunelle?" Welles was a large man.

Brunelle hesitated. He wasn't wearing gloves, but again they weren't looking for fingerprints. And he wasn't going to be sticking his fingers into any holes. He could wash his hands.

Once the body was rotated back enough, Donovan peered under and counted. "One, two, three. Okay, we can roll him back again."

Brunelle was happy to oblige. He knew what the disparity in the number of bullet holes meant. He also could distinguish between the clean round holes in the front of the body and the ragged torn holes on the back.

"Anterior," Donovan answered Brunelle's question. "He was shot four times in the front. Three of the bullets exited out the back." He patted Welles's bloated gut. "I expect I'll find the fourth one lodged in something hard and wet."

Brunelle winced. "I don't want you to think I'm saying this because we were friends, because we weren't. But when you testify, can you act a little less," he sought the best word, "flippant? A man was murdered. The jury is going to expect people to take that seriously."

Donovan frowned, but deflected Brunelle's question. "Testify?" he asked. "You think this will go to trial?"

Brunelle nodded. "Probably. The easy ones plead guilty. It's the hard cases that go to trial. And it's always easier for me when they're shot in the back."

CHAPTER 3

Trials were even harder if you didn't have a defendant to prosecute. Impossible, actually. But identifying a suspect wasn't Brunelle's job. It was Chen's. Luckily, Chen was good at his job.

"Got 'm," Chen announced when Brunelle answered his call that afternoon.

There was something about the way Chen had said that first word. The vagueness of the vowel after the 't'.

"Got him?" Brunelle asked, "or got them?"

He could practically hear Chen smile over the phone. "Them. Two suspects. Or rather, one suspect and one witness. Depends on who pulled the trigger."

"You haven't figured that out yet?" Brunelle asked.

"We're about to," Chen assured. "We've got them both downtown, separate holding cells, ready for interrogation. I thought you might want to watch."

The corner of Brunelle's mouth twitched. He refrained from making a 'You know I like to watch' joke, but he couldn't stop himself from smiling at it just the same. "I'll be there in ten minutes."

"We'll wait for you," Chen confirmed. "Bring popcorn. This could get good."

* * *

"How'd you I.D. them?" Brunelle asked Chen when he arrived at Seattle P.D.'s downtown precinct. They knew he was coming. A uniformed officer greeted him in the secure lobby and escorted him inside to the interrogation rooms.

"It's a brave new world, Dave," Chen answered. "There are cameras everywhere."

"I think that was '1984'," Brunelle put in. "But I get your meaning."

"You're right," Chen confirmed. "Wrong dystopia. Either way, the one we're living in now has video cameras in the lobby and more across the street. The one inside showed Welles letting two males into the building at 11:16 p.m. and those same two males running out of the building at 11:32."

"That's not a lot of time," Brunelle observed.

"Long enough, apparently," Chen said. "The camera across the street got the license plate. We ran the registration, got an address, and found them both still there. I've got somebody writing up the warrant to search the place. Maybe we'll get lucky and they were stupid enough not to throw the gun into Elliott Bay the moment they got outside."

Brunelle smiled slightly at the thought. His cases would all be a lot harder if defendants always did the smart thing.

"Where are they now?" Brunelle asked.

"We separated them," Chen explained. "Classic Prisoner's Dilemma."

"Literally." Brunelle nodded.

The Prisoner's Dilemma was a thought experiment where two accomplices are separated and questioned separately. If they both shut up, they both walk out the door, but if one of them blames the other and the other remains silent, then the talker walks and the silent one takes the fall. So the dilemma is, do you lawyer up, knowing that your fate depends on what your accomplice does? Do you trust him?

In Brunelle's experience, most suspects talked, regardless of what their accomplices were likely to do. Remaining silent in the face of police questioning took a level of resolve most criminals lacked when confronted by authorities; there was a reason crime increased when the sun went away. It was also against human nature. People like to talk. And to be heard. And understood. And when in trouble, everyone tries to talk their way out of it. Brunelle had no expectation that the two suspects would weigh the calculus of The Prisoner's Dilemma. He just figured they'd both confess to everything they both did, because that's what criminals did.

Most of them, anyway.

Half of them, it turned out.

"Maximillian Strunk," Chen pointed through the glass at the suspect seated at the table in Interrogation Room #1. He was young—nineteen or twenty by Brunelle's estimate—with a shaved head and tattoos creeping up out of the neck of his dirty t-shirt. His arms were thin but muscular. His eyes were ringed in dark circles and he couldn't keep his hands still.

"Looks guilty," Brunelle deadpanned. They were in an attached observation room, watching Strunk through a two-way mirror. Chen would go inside to question the suspect and Brunelle would hang back and watch. It wasn't his job to ask the suspect questions—not until he became the defendant and was stupid enough to take the stand at his trial.

"Agreed," Chen answered. "Too bad we can't just have

the jury take one look at them and vote on their initial gut reaction."

But Brunelle shook his head. "Nah. The defense bar would dress them up in argyle sweater vests and pastel pants. Whatever the game is, they figure out how to play it."

"I suppose you're right," Chen conceded. "Come on. Take a look at the other guy.

Where Strunk had been hard and wiry, Jonathan Beckle was soft and marshmallowy. He had loose curly hair that already needed a haircut, a round frame, and wide eyes that seemed to be trying to keep up with his expansive gut. Strunk looked angry. Beckle looked scared.

"He's gonna talk," Brunelle opined, almost sneering at the young man, barely over eighteen years old himself. "Shit, he might start before you even get in there. He looks like he's about to pop."

Chen nodded. "That was my initial appraisal as well. But that's why I'm going to start with Strunk. Let this guy stew in his own juices a bit more. If Strunk lawyers up, then we hit Beckle, get the story, and come back. If Strunk talks, there's no way this guy doesn't crumble."

"A sound plan," Brunelle approved. "I'll look forward to watching."

Brunelle had hurried to the precinct for the show, but that didn't mean he wasn't going to stop at the coffee cart in the courthouse lobby on his way out. He took his afternoon mocha and settled into one of the chairs in Observation Room #1. Looking at Strunk, Brunelle already felt pretty confident who pulled the trigger. Brunelle would flip Beckle and the doughy young man would become his star witness. Snitches might get stitches, but that happened after the snitching. It wouldn't be

Brunelle's problem.

"Mr. Strunk," Chen boomed as he suddenly entered the interrogation room, a junior detective trailing behind. Strength in numbers, plus a training opportunity. "I'm Detective Chen. I'd like to talk with you about what happened at the office of attorney William Harrison Welles."

"I had to do it, man." Strunk threw his hands up, sending ripples up those strong arms. "I didn't want to, but he made me do it. I had to protect Jonny, man. I had no choice."

Brunelle frowned, for several reasons. First, both he and Chen had completely misjudged Strunk. If anyone was scared and about to pop, it was that guy. Second, that meant their appraisal of Beckle was perhaps also off. But third, and the largest contributor to the frown, was what Maximillian Strunk was about to say, and how hard that was going to make his job.

"No choice?" Chen raised a dubious eyebrow. "Well, we'll see about that. Why don't you back up and start at the beginning? You were there the night he died, I take it?"

Strunk nodded profusely. "Yeah, man, we were there. We were totally there. Jonny needed a lawyer 'cause—" He hesitated, gears turning behind those smudge-rimmed eyes—"well, he just needed a lawyer, you know? And this guy, what's his name? Welles? Yeah, Welles. He was supposed to be like one of the best. And Jonny liked the best, you know, man?"

Chen shook his head. "No, I don't know. But tell me." He sat down across the table from Strunk. The junior detective remained standing. "Why did Jonny need the best lawyer? Was he in some sort of trouble?"

Strunk shifted in his seat. "I mean, yeah? I guess so? I don't know. He just told me he was gonna see some lawyer and he wanted me to come along. He said he didn't trust the guy. He was good, but he didn't trust him."

Brunelle nodded. Beckle was a good judge of character.

"Is that why you brought a gun along?" Chen ventured. It was risky to push too hard too soon, but years of experience had taught him to detect small openings, and push on them.

Strunk took a moment, then dropped his gaze and sighed. "Yeah, man. Jonny seemed really serious, so I knew what that meant. Shit might go down. And if shit was gonna go down, I needed to be ready. You know?"

Chen grunted noncommittally. "Shit went down, obviously," he said. "Otherwise you and I wouldn't be here right now talking about it. But let's take it one step at a time. What time did you get there?"

"That was another thing." Strunk extended a large, tattooed hand at the detective. "Who goes to meet a lawyer at ten at night?"

Depends on the lawyer, Brunelle supposed.

"So, ten p.m.," Chen confirmed. "Was anyone else there or was it just the three of you?"

"Just the three of us, man," Strunk answered. "The main entrance to the building was locked, right? It's not a great neighborhood already, and it was after dark, so I get it, man. But Jonny had to call him on his cell when we got there, and then he came down and let us in."

"Did you notice anything unusual about how he was acting?" Chen asked. The question seemed designed to keep the conversation going, but Brunelle knew it was also intended to start undermining the coming claim of self-defense Strunk had telegraphed. If Welles wasn't acting right, maybe they should have known better than to do whatever they did to set him off.

"He had a drink in his hand," Strunk answered. "I

remember that. But no, he was just normal, I guess. I mean, I don't know what a lawyer who meets with people late at night is supposed to act like, you know? I'm not saying I've never been in trouble, but my lawyers were always public defenders and public defenders don't work past five, man."

Brunelle knew that wasn't true. The public defenders probably worked the longest hours. In fact, it had gotten so bad the State Supreme Court actually passed court rules to limit their caseloads. No one was quite as exploitable as a government employee who chose their career based on a passion to help others. Just ask the teachers.

"So you went up to his office?" Chen continued.

Strunk nodded. "Yeah. Took the elevator. It was this cool open cage thing that rattled all the way up to the top floor." He smiled at the memory, exposing a missing canine, but the smile faded. "And then he led us inside his office."

"Nice office?" Chen asked. He wanted to keep the conversation going. It would also confirm he'd actually been inside.

Strunk gave an appraising shrug. "Yeah. I guess so. There was like a nice rug."

A nice blood-soaked rug, Brunelle amended silently.

"So what happened next?" Chen continued. "Did your buddy explain why he wanted to hire a lawyer?"

"I think so," Strunk frowned slightly, "but I didn't really listen in, you know? I was there to support him, but not to know what kind of trouble he was in."

"Wouldn't you want to know how much trouble he was in before you decided if you were going to support him?" Chen asked.

Strunk cocked his head at Chen. "Do you even have

friends, man?"

Brunelle couldn't suppress a laugh. He hoped the two-way mirror was soundproof.

"Let's focus on you, Max," Chen avoided answering the question. "What did you do if you weren't listening to their conversation?"

"So, there was like this table and chairs on the other side of the office, right?" Strunk explained. "I went over there and put in my earbuds to just like surf on my phone."

Brunelle recalled that table and chairs. Strunk had definitely been inside Welles's office.

"Oh yeah," Chen tried to sound like he knew what the kids these days were doing. "The Tic-Tac, right?"

Strunk laughed out loud himself. "TikTok, man. It's called TikTok. I don't even know what the fuck a Tic-Tac is."

Brunelle wondered whether Chen would explain it was a breath mint from the 1980s. He didn't think that would help matters.

"TikTok," Chen repeated instead. "Okay, yeah, sure. I guess I don't really care what you were doing when you weren't paying attention. When did you notice something wasn't right?"

Strunk took a moment, his mouth twisted into a knot. "I was just sitting there, right? And then all of a sudden I heard shouting, so I looked over and that lawyer guy was coming right over the desk at Jonny. His face was bright red and he was screaming something I couldn't even understand."

"What was Jonny doing?" Chen asked.

"He was, like, backing up," Strunk answered. "Trying to get away from the dude."

"What did you do?"

"I pulled my earbuds out and ran over there," Strunk said.

"I was like, what's going on, but the lawyer dude had totally lost it, man. He was screaming at Jonny, calling him a fucking liar and a bunch of other shit."

"What other shit?" Chen pressed. "It might be important."

Strunk thought for a minute. "I'm not sure, man. He called him a fucking liar. And, how dare you threaten me? You don't know who you're fucking with. And, oh yeah, then he said, I'll teach you to come to my office and say that to me. I definitely remember that one."

"Why that one?" Chen asked.

"'Cause, um, that's when he pulled the gun out of his desk."

Fuck. Brunelle frowned. He wasn't surprised, but he let himself be disappointed.

"The gun?" Chen repeated.

"Yeah, a gun," Strunk confirmed. "Shiny little semi-auto thing. He pointed it Jonny and started screaming at us to get out."

That's good, Brunelle thought. Welles didn't try to shoot them. He just wanted them to leave.

"And then, um, he just pulled the trigger," Strunk added.

And fuck again. But Brunelle wasn't as worried as he might have been. The words Strunk was saying were building a self-defense case, but his affect wasn't selling it. His voice was shaky, his cadence faltering. Brunelle wasn't sure Strunk was lying, but he wasn't sure he wasn't either.

"He pulled the trigger?" Chen confirmed. "Are you sure?"

That would leave evidence, Brunelle and Chen both knew. A bullet in either Jonny or the wall behind him. A shell casing on the floor. Gunshot residue on Welles's hand. Strunk may not have known any of that. He just knew he needed Welles to shoot first.

"Oh yeah, I'm totally sure," Strunk assured. "That's why I pulled out my gun and shot back. To protect Jonny."

Correction. Not self-defense. Defense of others. But they were both 'get out of jail free' cards. You can kill someone who's trying to kill you. You can also kill someone who's trying to kill someone else.

"How many times did you shoot?" Chen probed. "And how far away were you?"

Again, physical evidence. They knew from the autopsy there were at least four shots, with three of the bullets coming to rest inside Welles's torso. That meant a fourth bullet lodged in the wall behind him. If Strunk said 'Once' or even 'Twice', they would know he was lying. But they'd know he was telling the truth if he said what he said next.

"Four. I shot four times." Strunk sounded certain about that, at least. "They say to shoot twice center mass, right? So I did that, but twice."

"So, we should have found five shell casings in the office?" Chen challenged.

Strunk's eyebrows knitted together. "I said I shot four times."

"And you said Welles shot one time," Chen reminded him. "You also said he had a semi-auto, so it would have ejected a casing too. Your four shots, plus his one, equals five casings."

"It was a revolver!" Strunk practically shouted. "He had a revolver. So, no casings."

Brunelle wanted to smile. Chen had caught him in a lie. It just would have been so much better if that had happened in front of the jury. But the jury was a long way away. They were still trying to figure out what happened. But after that rather significant change in his story, Brunelle knew Strunk was lying.

"A revolver?" Chen crossed his arms. "Now it was a revolver?"

"It was always a revolver, man," Strunk said. "I swear. I, I just got confused. Said the wrong word. It was a revolver."

"We didn't find a revolver in his office, Max," Chen leaned forward. "We didn't find any guns in his office at all."

Strunk nodded rapidly. "Right, right. I know, I know. That's 'cause, um, we grabbed it. I grabbed it. I grabbed his gun. The revolver. On our way out. After I shot him, I grabbed the gun and we ran away. Uh, and then we got rid of the gun, man."

"How did you get rid of it?" Chen asked. "Where is it now?"

Brunelle wondered if they could find a single gun thrown into Elliott Bay. It was 50 feet deep immediately off the end of the pier. 100 feet deep if Strunk had a good arm, which it looked like he did. The odds weren't good.

"Uh, we just, like, sold it to some dude on the street."

Brunelle frowned. The odds of finding it from some random dude on the street were even worse.

"Some dude?" Chen repeated.

"Yeah, yeah." Strunk seemed to be convincing himself. He also seemed to appreciate the utility of his answer. "Just some dude."

"Both guns?" Chen pressed.

"Uh..." Strunk hesitated. His eyes darted back and forth.

"We're executing a search warrant on your apartment, Max," Chen advised him. "Are we going to find the guns there?"

"Um, we only sold the revolver," Strunk claimed.

"The revolver?" Chen shook his head. "We're going to

find your gun at your apartment, but you sold the victim's gun to some random guy on the street."

"Yeah." Strunk thought for a moment, then added another, "Yep."

Chen pinched the bridge of his nose. "Why would you get rid of his gun? That would have been the best evidence you're telling me the truth."

"I am telling you the truth," Strunk insisted. "Really. I promise. That's what happened, man. He pulled out a gun and, and he, um, shot at Jonny, and so I had to shoot, and I only shot four times, and we grabbed the guns, I mean, I did, I grabbed the gun, his gun, and we got the fuck out of there, man. That's what happened. Seriously, man. That's what happened. You gotta believe me."

Chen frowned and crossed his arms again. He shook his head slightly. "No, Max. I don't have to believe you."

Strunk's eyes widened. "But do you, man? Do you believe me?"

Brunelle didn't. Except for the part about shooting Welles to death. That seemed fairly well supported by the physical evidence.

Chen didn't answer Strunk's question. Instead, he stood up and told him, "We're going to talk to Jonny now."

Strunk's eyes flashed wide again, but then he nodded, almost to himself. He'd done his part.

It was time to see how the other prisoner handled his dilemma.

"I want a lawyer," Jonathan Beckle said as soon as Chen and his detective trainee walked into Interrogation Room #2. His voice didn't waver like Strunk's had when he'd detailed the shooting, but it wasn't entirely confident either. "I'm not talking with you until I've talked to a lawyer."

Chen stopped in his tracks and sighed through his nose. He knew the rules. Brunelle did too. The interrogation was over. As soon as a suspect asked for a lawyer, all questioning had to cease. Or if it didn't, if a cop asked questions anyway, none of the responses would be admissible in court. Beckle's defense attorney would move to suppress. In fact, he wouldn't even have to. Brunelle would have an ethical duty to suppress the statements themselves. He couldn't use evidence obtained in violation of a suspect's constitutional rights. And Chen wasn't about to violate Beckle's rights anyway.

He was still irritated. "Your buddy Max didn't mind talking to us," he told him.

Chen was planting a seed of doubt. The only way Chen could talk to Beckle now was if Beckle initiated the contact, and expressed, clearly and unequivocally that he didn't want a lawyer after all.

"I'm sure whatever Max said is the truth and exactly what happened." Beckle crossed his arms and looked away. "Now, I want my lawyer."

"You can get your own lawyer," Chen answered. "I don't have to get you a lawyer; I just can't talk to you without one. If you change your mind, let the guard know."

"Guard?" Beckle swung his head back to the detective.

"You're a prime suspect in a homicide," Chen explained. "You're not going home tonight. You're going to jail. And tomorrow you're going in front of a judge to face whatever charges the Prosecutor's Office decides to bring against you. It might be a long time before you feel the sun on your face again, Jonny."

Beckle tried to keep a poker face, but Brunelle had seen that particular move enough times to notice the slight quiver of Beckle's chin. Still, he held firm.

"I'll see what my lawyer has to say about all of that."

Chen didn't reply. Instead, he nodded at the guard by the door, who responded by stepping over to Beckle and pulling him to his feet. Beckle was going to a cell in the King County Jail. Chen went into Observation Room #2.

"I fucking hate lawyers," Chen growled as he entered, sneering through the glass at the exiting form of Beckle and his guard.

"Present company excepted?" Brunelle prompted.

But Chen just grumbled again. "Can you charge that Beckle asshole? I really don't want him to walk out the door tomorrow morning."

Brunelle frowned. "I'm going to have to look at the crime scene reports again. I can definitely charge Strunk. He admitted to shooting Welles and I bet I can use the physical evidence to poke enough holes in his defense of others claim to support a murder charge. But Beckle…" He put a hand to his chin. "I'm not sure I even want to charge him."

"What?" Chen almost barked. "Why not?"

"If he's a defendant, he has the right to remain silent," Brunelle said what they already both knew, "but if he's just a witness, I can force him to testify."

The Prisoner's Dilemma had played out to plan. Beckle kept his mouth shut and would walk out the door. And Strunk was in deep trouble.

CHAPTER 4

Arraignments were for defendants, not witnesses. That meant the next day, Jonathan Beckle was released from the King County Jail and Maximillian Strunk was brought, handcuffed and leg-chained, to the Criminal Presiding Courtroom where the day's arraignments were held. Every defendant arrested the previous day for a new felony would be brought before the judge, one after another, to be formally advised of the charges against them, enter a plea of not guilty, and have bail set. It was an assembly line of criminality: car theft, robbery, burglary, even murder. Car theft arraignments were a daily event. Robbery and burglary were almost as common. But murders, mercifully, were not an everyday event. When David Brunelle, homicide prosecutor, walked into the Presiding Courtroom, everyone knew why he was there.

"You're like the Angel of Death," came a voice from the corner. It was Jessica Edwards, senior attorney with the King County Public Defender's Office, seated against the wall, legs crossed, a stack of new case files on her lap. "When you show up, one person's already dead and you're here to try to take the life away from someone else."

"Justice?" Brunelle replied. "Did you mean to say, when I show up, a killer is going to face justice?"

Edwards held a tight smile and shook her head slightly. "No, Dave. That is definitely not what I meant to say."

"Hm," Brunelle replied. He reached into his case file and extracted a copy of the criminal complaint. He handed it to Edwards. "You might change your mind when you see who the victim is."

Edwards frowned, then took the paper and scanned for the name. "William Harrison Welles?" she gasped. "Welles is dead?"

"Welles was murdered," Brunelle clarified. "One of yours. So, maybe I'm seeking justice after all."

Edwards's frown deepened, and changed its shade. "It's still just revenge, Dave, not justice. Even if the victim was a defense attorney." She looked again at the complaint in her hand. "I can't believe Bill is dead."

Bill. Brunelle had never heard anyone call him that. Then again, he didn't really travel in their circles.

"So, I take it, Mr. Strunk isn't in your stack of files?" Brunelle pointed at the files on Edwards's lap. Her cases for the afternoon.

"No." Edwards shook her head. "I would have noticed that one."

Brunelle nodded and turned to scan the courtroom for any private attorneys who might have been retained to represent Strunk. He was an interesting character. Tough-looking and gun-toting, but he seemed in good health and had a smartphone to look at the Tic-Tac on. He might come from a good family, or at least one with resources.

"Dave?" Edwards drew his attention back to her. She handed him the complaint back. "I still think it's revenge, not justice, but… go ahead and get some revenge for us."

Brunelle offered a half-smile as he took the complaint back. He'd do his best. But he was anxious to know who his opponent would be. Judging by Edwards's reaction, it would have to be somebody willing to put money over tribalism. The defense bar was more than a profession; it was a calling. They treated it almost like a religion. They had to. No one could spend a career trying to put criminals back out on the streets without believing in some higher good, even if it was just a lie they told themselves to be able to fall asleep at night. And like any mass delusion, the fellow deluded were necessary to keep a person from seeing the truth and dropping criminal defense for a more lucrative field like family law.

That was how Brunelle spotted his opponent. It wasn't just that he was wearing far too expensive a suit for the dirty world of criminal law. It was that he was wearing too expensive of a suit and Brunelle didn't recognize him. Every criminal defense attorney in town would feel the same as Edwards; none of them would want the case. It had to be someone who wasn't part of the Sacred Order of Criminal Defense Martyrs. It had to be someone like—

"Nathaniel Ryder." The young lawyer in the too expensive suit extended his hand as Brunelle traversed the crowd of other attorneys waiting for court to begin. "You must be the prosecutor on the Strunk matter."

Brunelle's mouth tightened. He supposed Ryder had been able to judge him as easily as Brunelle had judged him. Brunelle's suit definitely wasn't too expensive, not on a government salary. He knew he looked like a prosecutor; he just wasn't sure he liked being reminded of it.

"Dave Brunelle." He shook Ryder's hand. They both had firm grips, not sweaty, not held too long. The first combat was a draw. "You represent Mr. Strunk, then?"

"That is correct." Ryder reached into the leather satchel he was carrying in lieu of the old school briefcase old men like Brunelle would have carried back in the day. Ryder appeared to be in his early 30s, clean shaven, with a salon haircut that showcased an athletic neck. He handed Brunelle proof of his representation. "My Notice of Appearance."

Brunelle accepted it. The bottom right corner held the name of Ryder's firm, one of the white-shoe civil firms in town. The ones who didn't touch criminal work.

"Devlin and Gray?" Brunelle read aloud. "I didn't know they handled criminal cases."

He did know. They didn't. So he was curious.

"I do." Ryder smiled, but not warmly.

"Strunk's daddy have money or something?" Brunelle asked. "Devlin and Gray can't be cheap."

The smile lost whatever minimal warmth it might have held. "I'm not about to discuss my retainer. Certainly not with opposing counsel. Let's focus on the merits of the case, Mr. Brunelle, or the lack thereof."

Fine by me, Brunelle thought. He nodded. "I'll see about getting us to go first."

Ryder may have had a fancy suit and a great haircut, but Brunelle had the connections. He'd been doing arraignments in that courtroom since Ryder was in middle school. He knew the bailiff and he knew how to get himself first in line. By the time the judge finally took the bench, Brunelle was already standing at the bar, ready to arraign Maximillian Strunk on the charge of murder.

The judge in question was The Honorable Helen Jacoby. She'd been a judge since Ryder was in elementary school. Maybe preschool. She'd spent most of her judicial career handling family law and juvenile matters because she was really, really good at it. But every now and again, everyone had to rotate into what they weren't comfortable with to make room for someone else to do their job worse than them. Still, it was nice to see a friendly face.

"Mr. Brunelle." She nodded down stoically at the prosecutor obviously ready to call the first case. Then she spied Ryder approaching the bar and her face lit up into a genuine smile. "Mr. Ryder! What a pleasant surprise. How's your father?"

Ah, Brunelle thought. It wasn't Strunk's father he needed to worry about; it was Ryder's. Brunelle could guess Nathaniel Ryder, Sr, had donated a tidy sum to Judge Jacoby's reelection efforts over the years. That was another thing white-shoe firms like Devlin and Gray specialized in.

"The Old Man is doing very well, Your Honor," Ryder replied warmly. "Thank you for asking. He sends his regards."

"Please send him mine as well, Mr. Ryder," the judge returned the warmth. "Which case are you here on?"

"The Strunk matter," Ryder answered. "Maximillian Strunk."

"Then we will handle that matter first," Jacoby said, before noticing Brunelle at the bar. "Is that your case as well, Mr. Brunelle?" There was no particular warmth in her voice when she addressed Brunelle.

"Yes, Your Honor," Brunelle confirmed. He didn't feel a need to add any geniality to his voice either. It was business. And he wasn't going to win an affection contest with the son of one of the judge's big donors anyway.

"Then, you may call the case, counsel," Judge Jacoby instructed with a raise of her chin.

Brunelle nodded to the guard at the door to the holding cells behind the courtroom. "The parties are ready on the matter of The State of Washington versus Maximillian Andrew Strunk."

The guard opened the security door with an audible 'clunk' and shouted, "Strunk!" into the depths. A few moments later, Strunk emerged, handcuffed, in red jail scrubs, but otherwise looking no worse for the wear of spending a night in jail. With the additional information from Ryder, Brunelle could see how Strunk looked both tough and weak. He projected the image of a street thug with a shaved head and tattoos, but he had a rich daddy who watched out for him. Just like Ryder.

Strunk took his place at the bar next to Ryder, who gave him a supportive pat on the back, then Brunelle began the arraignment.

Arraignments were simple enough. They were designed to give the defendant formal notice of the exact charges against them. There wasn't much to it, except to file the criminal complaint, ask if they understood the charges, and enter a plea of not guilty. Even if a defendant wanted to plead guilty, they weren't going to be allowed to do it at the arraignment calendar. There were thirty other defendants waiting their turn and only three hours until lunch. Guilty pleas involved a 12-page form and a lengthy colloquy between the judge and the defendant about all of the constitutional rights they were giving up. The lawyerly equivalent of, 'Are you sure you want to do this? Really?' A guilty plea could easily take 30 minutes. An arraignment took two.

Ryder having accepted the defense copies of the complaint, waived formal reading of the complaint in open court, and entered a plea of not guilty to the charge of murder in the first degree, the judge turned to the part of the hearing that really mattered: the bail hearing.

"I will hear first from the State regarding conditions of release," she invited Brunelle.

"Thank you, Your Honor," he began. "The State asks the Court to set bail in the amount of one million dollars. This is a murder case. The defendant fled the scene and, by his own admission, destroyed evidence in immediate flight from the murder. He is facing a significant prison sentence if convicted. The State therefore believes he is a flight risk and has already shown a propensity not to follow the law and to interfere with the proper functioning of the judicial system. One million dollars is consistent with bail set in similar cases and there is nothing particular to this case or this defendant which would warrant a lower bail. Thank you."

Jacoby gave a curt, pursed lipped nod to Brunelle and then turned to smile at defense counsel.

"Mr. Ryder?" she invited.

"Thank you very much, Your Honor." Ryder returned the smile. "Mr. Brunelle misleads the Court when he says there is nothing particular about this case which would warrant a lower bail than typical for a murder case."

Brunelle raised an eyebrow. He wasn't accustomed to being accused of misconduct, at least not so early in the case. He was reminded that Ryder was from a civil firm. Accusations of misconduct against opposing counsel were common currency in the civil world. In the criminal world, there was a code of honor amongst the lawyers. Everyone was doing their job to the best of their ability. Accusations of misconduct were serious. It wasn't just money they were arguing over; it was someone's life. If you were going to accuse a prosecutor of violating someone's rights or a defense attorney of violating their duty to their client, you better have something to back it up. And you usually brought it up first directly to them, off the record. Not in open court in your first official sentence after, 'Thank you, Your Honor.'

"This is not a murder case, Your Honor," Ryder continued. "This is a self-defense case. Or rather, more specifically, a case of defense of others. Mr. Strunk acted to save the life of his longtime friend, Jonathan Beckle. While the result of his actions is something we can all agree is tragic, those actions themselves were lawful. Indeed, I am shocked the State has even brought charges against Mr. Strunk. He told them what happened, explained how he had no choice but to protect another human being from imminent harm, but nevertheless he now finds himself before Your Honor, handcuffed like a common criminal, facing, as Mr. Brunelle threatened just now, a lengthy prison sentence, all for conduct which, under our law and long-established traditions, was not criminal."

He put his hand on Strunk's shoulder again.

"Mr. Strunk stands before Your Honor not only willing to come to court and contest these charges, but eager to do so. He has retained counsel at no small expense to himself and his family, and he has done so with the express intent to vindicate himself and his actions in a court of law. He is not a flight risk and he is not a threat to anyone who isn't about to shoot a friend in his immediate presence, a circumstance he sincerely hopes will never happen again. Bail is not necessary in this case, Your Honor. We would respectfully request that the Court release Mr. Strunk on his personal recognizance. He will appear for court and he will win this case. Thank you."

Jacoby turned again, a disapproving scowl directed at Brunelle.

"Is that correct, Mr. Brunelle? Is this a defense of others case?" she asked. "And do you have any response to that assertion or how it impacts the question of bail?"

"This is a murder case," Brunelle replied, stiffening his back a bit. "The defendant has claimed that he was acting to defend another person, but he did so after fleeing the scene, disposing of evidence, and having to be tracked down and arrested by law enforcement. In a murder case, there are really only two defenses: either it wasn't me, or I had to do it. In this case, Mr. Strunk can hardly claim it wasn't him because he did it in front of a witness who knows and can identify him. That leaves, I had to do it. Self-defense. Or in this case, defense of others. I have encountered this defense before, Your Honor, and I expect to encounter it again. Nothing about what the defendant claimed after he got caught makes this case exceptional. We would again ask the Court to set bail in the amount of one million dollars."

Jacoby frowned. He wasn't sure if it was in response to his argument, or an unconscious expression of thinking as she decided what to do. Probably both, he supposed.

"Today is not the day to judge the merits of the case," she began. Brunelle liked that beginning. "But neither can I ignore completely the facts underpinning the charges and the defense to be argued later." Brunelle liked that less. "Every case must be weighed individually and that would not occur if bail were set solely on the nature of the charges brought, regardless of the defenses thereto. Mr. Ryder makes a persuasive argument. I have little concern that, having availed himself of Mr. Ryder's services, Mr. Strunk would then flee the jurisdiction. I do believe he wishes to have his day in court and therefore will return if released."

Brunelle really disliked that.

"However—"

Brunelle liked the placement of that 'however'.

"—this is a murder case. The charges are serious and the penalty if convicted is significant. I cannot discount completely the risk that, once released, Mr. Strunk might not reevaluate the situation and decide his better fortunes lie somewhere other than our courthouse. I do not think I can quite bring myself to release someone accused of murder on their own recognizance. Some bail is warranted. But one million dollars is unnecessary. I will set bail in the amount of one hundred thousand dollars."

Brunelle shook his head. She might as well have PR'd him. If Daddy Strunk could hire Devlin and Gray, he could post $100K.

"Thank you, Your Honor," Ryder chimed in a tone that confirmed Strunk would be home in time for dinner.

"Thank you, Your Honor," Brunelle echoed, if only because that was the professional thing to do, and he knew he'd be in front of Jacoby again on a different case soon enough.

Brunelle stepped away from the bar to let the next case be called and the guards led Strunk back to the cells, if only to wait while the bail was posted and his release was processed. Ryder said a few parting words to his client, then found Brunelle trying to leave the courtroom without talking to him.

"Looks like I won the first round," Ryder beamed as he caught up to Brunelle at the door to the hallway.

"I can't argue with that," he answered, "but it's a long fight."

"May the best lawyer win." Ryder grinned.

"Nah." Brunelle shook his head. "May justice win."

CHAPTER 5

Justice couldn't win by itself, of course. It would need help from Brunelle. And Brunelle wasn't too proud to admit he'd need help too.

"Gwendolyn Elizabeth Carlisle," he greeted his fellow prosecutor from the doorway of her office.

Carlisle looked up. "That's not actually my middle name."

Brunelle shrugged. "It was a guess. Can I come in?"

"Do you want to know my real middle name?"

"Not really," Brunelle answered. He stepped in and took a seat across the desk from her. "I have a proposition for you."

"The Welles case?" Carlisle ventured.

Brunelle surrendered a nervous grin. "How'd you know?"

"Everyone's talking about it," Carlisle said. "Big time defense attorney ends up shot to death in his office? That's going to spread like wildfire in a Prosecutor's Office. I also heard you were the D.A. on call. Two meet two. I take it I'm four?"

Brunelle squinted at the math metaphor. It didn't seem

quite right, but he decided to go with it. "Uh, sure. Yeah, I want co-counsel on this one. I just met the defense attorney and he's definitely going to have some resources behind him."

"Devlin and Gray." Carlisle nodded. "I already looked it up."

"Right," Brunelle confirmed. "So, I figure we owe it to good ol' Welles to do our best to avenge his murder."

Carlisle cocked her head at him for a moment. "Really?"

"Nah." Brunelle laughed. "I just want to win. And like you said, everyone's talking about it."

"And you think your best chance of winning is if I second-chair, huh?" Carlisle smiled. "Thanks, Dave."

"Well, that," Brunelle agreed, "and also, if I lose, I'll have someone to share the blame."

Carlisle's smile faded. Then she stood up and pulled her coat off the back of her door. "Come on."

"Where are we going?" Brunelle asked, following her to his feet.

"The crime scene," Carlisle answered. "I want to see it before the cops leave and let the cleaning staff ruin it."

* * *

Welles's office looked largely the same as when Brunelle had seen it approximately 36 hours earlier. The crime scene tape was still up, but Carlisle had been right to hurry. There was a single cop standing guard, and he looked more than ready to get back to the streets.

Brunelle flashed his prosecutor I.D. badge as they approached. Carlisle didn't bother.

"I know who you are," the officer responded.

Brunelle took some satisfaction in that.

"You're Gwen Carlisle, from the D.A.'s Office." He

pointed to her, then to Brunelle. "And you're the prosecutor who came out to the scene that night."

"Brunelle," he was annoyed at having to inform the officer, especially since he knew Carlisle's name. "We need to take a look around again."

"Fine by me." The officer shrugged and picked a clipboard up from where it was leaning against the wall. "Just sign in on the crime scene log. I'm just waiting for Detective Chen to tell me I can take the crime scene tape down. Forensics finished up late yesterday. Not much left to see in there anymore, I'm thinking."

"Thanks, Dan," Carlisle replied. "I just need to take a quick look with my own eyes."

"Of course. I totally understand." He took the signed clipboard back from the prosecutors and gestured toward the interior of the office. "What wonders await you within?"

Carlisle entered first, with Brunelle grumbling behind her.

"How'd you know him?" he had to ask.

"You get to know a lot of people doing this job," Carlisle answered. "Especially cops. It's good to remember people's names. Best way to make friends in case you need to ask a favor later."

Brunelle shrugged. "I suppose so."

"You still don't want to know my middle name?" Carlisle joked. "In case you need a favor from me some day?"

"I already got my favor from you," Brunelle answered. "That's why we're here."

"Fair enough," Carlisle replied. Then she lowered her head and walked purposefully into the center of Welles's office.

Brunelle followed her and glanced around, hands in his

pockets. The officer was right. There wasn't much left to see. Forensics had collected everything that might have had some evidentiary value. At least everything they suspected might have value. One of the challenges was trying to figure that out before a suspect was apprehended and questioned. They knew to take the blood-soaked rug, but what might they have overlooked because they didn't know to look for it?

"Is this where the body was?" Carlisle pointed at a large dark discoloration in the wood floor, right in front of Welles's mammoth desk.

"Yeah," Brunelle confirmed. "There was a rug, but they must have collected it."

"Is this where Strunk said Welles was standing when he shot him?" Carlisle followed up.

Brunelle took a moment to try to recall. "I remember he said Welles was 'coming over his desk' at Beckle. That wording was unique. Really painted a picture, you know? But then he said Welles reached into his desk drawer and pulled out a gun after that." He looked again at the desk, and where the stain on the floor was. "I don't think he could have reached back that far from where he was found."

"I don't think so either," Carlisle agreed. "Good. One point for us. Did he say whether Welles got off a shot?"

Brunelle nodded. "One shot, he said. Didn't hit either of them."

"Which means it hit the wall behind them." Carlisle strode over to the wall opposite Welles's desk. She craned her neck up, down, and all around, examining the wall, but careful not to touch it. "I don't see any bullet strikes at all. Two points for us."

Brunelle smiled. He liked the game. And that they were

winning.

"Shell casings?" Carlisle asked.

"Strunk said he fired four times," Brunelle answered, "and four casings were recovered."

"No casing for Welles's shot?" Carlisle deduced. "Three points."

But Brunelle shook his head. "He claimed it was a revolver."

"And revolvers don't eject their casings," Carlisle knew. "Smart."

"Not that smart," Brunelle said. "He said it was a semi-auto first, then changed it to revolver after Chen told him there weren't enough casings."

Carlisle considered for a moment. "I'll give us a half-point for that obvious lie. Where's this alleged revolver now?"

"Allegedly sold to some random guy on the street immediately after the murder," Brunelle told her.

"That's a good story," Carlisle admired. "We'd never find that guy."

"Especially since it's complete bullshit," Brunelle added.

"Did he sell his own gun that way too?" Carlisle asked.

"No, that one was found in his apartment when they executed the search warrant," Brunelle answered. "Ballistics will do the formal match, but he already admitted to shooting him, so it's not like we need that."

"Won't hurt either." Carlisle shrugged. "What was his excuse for selling the victim's gun but not the murder weapon?"

"I'm not sure he gave a specific excuse," Brunelle recalled, "but his general presentation suggested 'I'm an idiot'."

"Probably true," Carlisle observed. "Jury might buy that."

"But it won't explain where Welles was standing when he

was shot," Brunelle pointed out, "or why there aren't any bullet holes in the opposite wall. We'll need to keep Officer Dan here a bit longer and have forensics come back out to properly document those things now that we have Strunk's statement."

Carlisle nodded, but didn't answer audibly. She put her own hands in her pockets and strolled around the room, stopping a moment to take in the view of the bay.

"Why were they even here?" she asked, turning back around. "Why did they go to see a criminal defense attorney at nearly midnight? Did one of them just get charged with a crime? Have an arraignment the next morning?"

Brunelle shook his head. "No. We ran them both. Neither of them had any recent arrests. Strunk has an M.I.P. from a few years back, but nothing else. Beckle is completely clean, not so much as a speeding ticket. Neither of them needed a criminal defense attorney."

"Then that's what we need to figure out," Carlisle concluded. "Why did they come to see one of Seattle's top defense attorneys? What did they want from William Harrison Welles?"

CHAPTER 6

The most direct way of discovering why Maximillian Strunk and Jonathan Beckle were in the office of William Harrison Welles that fateful night was to ask them directly. The problem with that was they had charged Strunk with murder and he therefore had a right to remain silent. In theory, his lawyer could allow him to talk to the prosecutors, but that would—and should—lead to him being disbarred for malpractice. That left Beckle. They hadn't had enough to charge Beckle. According to what evidence they did have, he was standing there when one man shot another man in his presence. Brunelle was sure there was more to it than that, but he couldn't prove it. Not yet.

The good news was that Beckle was released from custody and became nothing more than a witness. And prosecutors could talk to witnesses.

The bad news was that witnesses could hire lawyers too.

Beckle worked at a small accounting firm in North Seattle. The Wallingford neighborhood, to be exact. An upscale neighborhood on the other side of the freeway from the University of Washington, filled with overpriced coffee shops among even more overpriced homes. It was hardly the place one would expect to find a murderer. But then again, Beckle was just a witness.

So far.

If they could tie him to whatever plans the two of them really had when they talked their way into seeing Welles so late that night, and if those plans involved committing any sort of felony against Welles, then Beckle could be charged with 'felony murder' for the actions of his accomplice. Since neither Beckle nor Strunk needed a criminal defense attorney when they went to see him, one working theory was that it was really a pretense to rob a flamboyant, successful, and therefore likely very rich attorney, late at night when no one else would be around to help him. Brunelle didn't have any evidence yet to back that theory up, but that was why they had come to see Beckle.

Maybe, having apparently been cleared of the murder and released, Beckle would let his guard down and talk to them.

Or maybe not.

There was only one way to find out.

Brunelle parked his car a few doors down from the converted house that served as the office for Dunlap & Dunlap Accountants. All of the houses on the street had been rezoned at some point from residential to light commercial, resulting in a series of what looked like single family homes but were actually small businesses like accountants, chiropractors, even a veterinarian clinic. None of them had parking, and the streets were barely the width of two cars, but Brunelle managed to jam his mid-sized sedan between two compacts. He and Carlisle emerged from the vehicle and made their way up the narrow sidewalk to the front door of Dunlap & Dunlap.

An electronic bell chimed at the opening of the door and

Beckle looked up from his spot at the reception desk. For a moment, Brunelle expected Beckle to recognize him but then he remembered that he'd watched the entire interrogation from the observation. Beckle had never seen him.

"Good afternoon," Beckle greeted them. "Welcome to Dunlap and Dunlap. Do you have an appointment with one of our team members?"

Very professional. Friendly even. You'd never guess he'd just witnessed a murder. Committed by his best friend, even.

"Not exactly." Brunelle reached for his I.D. "We were hoping to meet with you actually."

"Me?" His expression dropped. There it was. The fear Brunelle had expected. And, if he was honest with himself, had wanted. "About what?"

"We're from the King County Prosecutor's Office," Carlisle explained, pulling her own wallet out of her back pocket. "We had a couple of que—"

"No!" Beckle slammed the top of his receptionist's desk. "I told the cops I'm not talking to anyone without a lawyer."

"Do you have a lawyer?" Brunelle called his bluff.

"As a matter of fact, I do." Or not.

Beckle reached for his wallet as well and extracted a business card. "Here. This is my lawyer."

Carlisle took it and read the name aloud. "Nathanial Ryder. Devlin and Gray, Attorneys at Law."

"That's Strunk's attorney," Brunelle said. "He can't represent both of them."

But Carlisle shrugged. "Depends. Right now, only one of them is charged with murder."

"Right now?" Beckle practically shrieked. "Is that a threat?"

"It's a fact," Brunelle answered. "And facts can change. Just because they let you walk out the next morning doesn't mean you aren't still in trouble."

"We can't talk to him, Dave." Carlisle placed a hand on his arm. "He's represented."

"Yeah, by the murderer's attorney," Brunelle complained. "It's bullshit."

"It's a bar complaint," Carlisle countered. "Don't think he won't do it. Those civil guys file bar complaints against each other like they've got a punch card for half off their bar dues."

"Civil guys?" Beckle repeated. "He doesn't do criminal cases?"

Brunelle grinned slightly. They weren't going to be able to talk to Beckle, but maybe Beckle would be talking to Ryder. They should circle back in a few days. Beckle might be unrepresented soon enough.

I'm sorry, Mr. Beckle," Brunelle offered a concerned frown. "My colleague is correct. If you have a lawyer, we have to communicate through him. It's too bad he also represents the one person who could change his story and get you arrested again. But that's between you two. Have a good day."

"Wait!" Beckle called out as they turned toward the door. When they turned back, Beckle seemed uncertain what to do. "Maybe I should talk to you. I don't know. What do you think I should do?"

"We can't give you legal advice Mr. Beckle," Carlisle answered. "That's Mr. Ryder's job. Goodbye."

They turned again toward the door. Beckle didn't try again to stop them as they exited onto the sidewalk.

"That didn't go very well," Brunelle observed.

Carlisle shrugged. "I don't know. We learned something.

Ryder is keeping tight control over the case. That suggests he's worried about what might come out."

"He should be," Brunelle answered. He jerked a thumb at the building they had just exited. "This just confirms Strunk was lying."

"Or there's more to the story," Carlisle suggested.

"You can lie by omission," Brunelle countered. "Strunk lied and Beckle is omitting."

He looked again at Dunlap & Dunlap and frowned. "I really don't like that guy. He's like a coward who's just brave enough to survive."

"The worst kind," Carlisle agreed. Then she pointed down the street. "Come on. There's a coffee shop a few blocks that way. Let's grab a couple of lattes and come up with next steps."

Brunelle was about to agree—he wasn't about to turn down afternoon coffee—when a woman burst out of Dunlap & Dunlap and called out to them. "Excuse me! Excuse me! Were you two just in my business? You really upset my receptionist."

Brunelle looked to Carlisle, who returned his expression. This woman, whoever she was, was almost certainly not represented by Nathaniel Ryder. They could talk to her.

"Oh, goodness. We're so sorry," Brunelle replied. "We didn't mean to upset anyone."

That he would have minded, but that wasn't necessarily their intention, so he was telling the truth.

"We're from the King County Prosecutor's Office," he explained further. "Mr. Beckle witnessed a murder the other day and we were hoping to speak with him about what he saw."

The woman in question was probably one of the Dunlaps, Brunelle supposed based on her claim that Beckle was her receptionist. She was probably approaching 50, wearing what passed for business attire in Seattle—pants and sweater—with shoulder length brown hair that could probably have been styled better.

"Oh dear." She put a hand to her throat. "So, that's what it is. Jonathan has been so quiet these last two days. He came in over two hours later yesterday and wouldn't talk about why."

He was in jail, Brunelle knew, but he didn't elucidate.

Instead he nodded his head. "Yes, it happened the night before. It was very tragic. One of his best friends has been arrested for the murder. I'm sure it's been difficult for him."

Ms. Probably-Dunlap shook her head empathetically. "Poor Jonathan. After all he's been through. And now this."

Another exchange of glances with Carlisle.

"All he's been through?" Carlisle repeated, inviting further explanation.

The woman frowned slightly and clicked her tongue. "I probably shouldn't tell you this," she said, getting ready to tell them that, "but you said you're the prosecutors, right? You're the good guys."

"I like to think so," Brunelle said.

Carlisle shot him a sharp look. "Yes, we're the good guys," she said. "We just want to help Jonathan."

Help him incriminate himself and his best friend, Brunelle thought.

"What has he been through?" Carlisle asked. "It might help us understand everything better. So we can do our jobs."

Because we're the good guys, Brunelle wanted to say. But he knew he needed to let Carlisle take over that particular conversation.

"Of course, of course," Ms. Dunlap—Brunelle was just

going to assume that was her name until and unless they learned otherwise—said. "It's just that he's worked so hard and come so far. I mean, he literally came from nothing."

Carlisle cocked her head very slightly. "Nothing?"

The woman offered a tight-lipped frown and a knowing nod. "He's an orphan. Raised in foster care. Do you know what the odds are that someone grows up in that kind of environment and never once gets in trouble with the law?"

Brunelle did know actually, and it wasn't as increased of a chance us people might think. Or as Ms. Dunlap obviously did think.

She laughed slightly and waved a hand at them. "Oh, well, of course you. You're prosecutors. You probably see all kinds of things people like me and my husband could never dream of."

Dunlap & Dunlap. Husband and wife. That checked out, Brunelle decided. They were definitely speaking with Ms. Dunlap.

"How did you know he was raised in foster care?" Carlisle asked. "Did he tell you that?"

Ms. Dunlap nodded. "Yes, although not at first or anything. That's not the sort of thing that comes up in a job interview. I'm not even sure you can ask things like that. Not that we would. I don't care about that. I just want employees who work hard and are good people." She smiled at them. "Like you."

Brunelle decided to jump in, if only to stop having to hear about how great he was. He didn't feel great allowing this woman to tell them secrets without mentioning that they really, really wanted to charge sweet little Jonathan Beckle with murder.

"Thank you, Ms. Dunlap," he said. "You've been very helpful."

"Oh, I'm not Mrs. Dunlap," the woman waved her hand at them again. "My name is Betty McFadden. My husband worked for the original Mr. Dunlap then bought the practice when he retired. We kept the name because it was already established. But don't feel bad. A lot of people make that same mistake."

Brunelle frowned. He didn't like making mistakes. Good guys weren't supposed to make mistakes. They also weren't supposed to trick nice older women who dish dirt on murder suspects. "Thank you, Ms. McFadden," he corrected. "Let's keep this little conversation between us for now, shall we? I would hate for Jonathan to be even more upset than he already is."

Betty McFadden gave Brunelle a wink. "Gotcha. Good idea. Thank you for talking with me.'

"One more thing," Carlisle interjected. Brunelle was ready to wrap it up, but he knew Carlisle wouldn't prolong the conversation without a good reason. "How long has Jonathan been working here?"

Ms. McFadden thought for a moment, then answered, "It'll be two years next month. Is that important?"

Carlisle shrugged a shoulder slightly. "It might be. Thank you for your time, Ms. McFadden. Jonathan is lucky to have a boss like you."

"Well, he's lucky to have two prosecutors like you working on his case," Ms. McFadden returned. "You have a job to do. I'm sure he knows why you're prosecuting his friend."

"Yes." Brunelle smiled sardonically. "I'm sure he does too."

CHAPTER 7

The visit to Beckle produced more questions than answers. Or more leads. Questions were annoying. Leads were interesting. Brunelle and Carlisle agreed they should dig more into Jonathan Beckle's past. But first, they had a court date to discuss Maximillian Strunk's future.

Between the arraignment and trial, every criminal case has several pretrial hearings. Shortly prior to the trial date was the Readiness Hearing, which was what it sounded like. The parties appeared in court so the judge could ask if they were ready for trial. Things could come up. Witnesses could have scheduling conflicts. Lab results could be backed up. The lawyers might just want some more time to negotiate if they were close to a plea bargain. The judge didn't want to summon a hundred jurors for a murder case only to find out it was going to be continued for a month because the defense attorney had vacation plans.

Prior to the Readiness Hearing there might be pretrial motions to suppress or limit evidence. Maybe the defendant confessed but the cop didn't read him his Miranda rights. Maybe they found the stolen goods in the defendant's house, but the search warrant was stale. Maybe, maybe, maybe. Defense attorneys were a creative bunch. They had to be. And if they got creative enough, the prosecutor could find themselves in front of a judge defending the police's actions and begging for their evidence not to be suppressed.

But before any of that, there was the first pretrial hearing, called simply the Pretrial Conference. It was the first opportunity after the arraignment for the attorneys to sit down and discuss the cases. Most criminal cases settled with some sort of plea bargain, and bargaining required conferencing with the other side. It could be a very productive hearing. Or the defendant could hire Nathaniel Ryder of Devlin & Gray.

"Mr. Brunelle," Ryder greeted him as Brunelle walked up to him in The Pit, the large conference room between the main criminal courtroom where all the pretrials were held. It was a little like the floor of the stock exchange. Most prosecutors and every public defender would have multiple cases set for pretrial conferences at the same time. The lawyers would then rotate around The Pit like the teacup ride at Disneyland, making offers and counteroffers in between small talk and sharing pictures of the kids or the latest vacation. Ryder, on the other hand, had only one case, and it was with Brunelle. And Carlisle.

Ryder nodded at Carlisle. "You already called for backup? I didn't think you'd panic so fast."

"I don't have an entire law firm at my disposal," Brunelle explained. "I've got better. This is my co-counsel, Gwen Carlisle."

Ryder pursed his lips as he appraised his new opponent. "You can bring in a dozen junior prosecutors, Brunelle. It won't change the fact that my client was acting in the defense of others. His actions were justified under the law and he's not guilty of murder."

"His story is bullshit," Carlisle spoke up.

"His story is the only evidence you have of what happened," Ryder pointed out.

"It doesn't match with the physical evidence," Carlisle said. "We don't have to prove exactly what happened. We have to prove he killed the victim and he confessed to that. Then we point out that the rest of his story simply can't be true, and then everyone in the courtroom will know he wasn't justified and he is guilty of murder."

Ryder crossed his arms. "You make it sound so simple."

"The truth is usually pretty simple," Carlisle said. "Maybe your guy would be interested in talking to us again, but this time he tells us the truth."

Ryder laughed. "You can't seriously believe I would let Mr. Strunk speak with you while he's under indictment for murder"

"I wasn't talking about Strunk," Carlisle said.

"Beckle," Brunelle put in. "We know you represent Beckle now too."

Ryder allowed a smile to unfurl on his smug lips. "I wondered when you'd discover that. Honestly, I was hoping it would be at trial, when you tried to call him as a witness."

"I don't plan on calling him as a witness," Brunelle said.

Ryder raised an eyebrow. "You don't?"

"I plan on him being a defendant by then," Brunelle explained. "And you know I can't call a defendant to the stand."

Ryder shook his head. "I don't really have time for all of this bravado, counselors. Mr. Beckle will not be charged because he will not speak to you. Mr. Strunk will be acquitted because he did talk to you."

Brunelle wanted to say, 'Says you!' but he knew it would likely be ineffectual. Instead, he decided to poke Ryder where it might actually hurt. Or at least where he was used to poking others.

"It seems like a conflict of interest to represent both Strunk and Beckle," Brunelle said. "What if one of them wants to rat out the other one?"

"I assure you, Mr. Brunelle, that will not be happening," Ryder answered. "And until and unless it does, there is no conflict of interest. Only a potential conflict of interest, which each of them has already waived, in writing. I know what I'm doing."

Brunelle doubted that, but he had to admit that Ryder exuded confidence, whether warranted or not.

"Look," Ryder said, "perhaps we could save ourselves some time and just agree to dismiss the case. Then we can all move on to other matters. Do you not have other cases? I know I do. And why are you going to fight so hard on a loser of a case when the alleged victim was a criminal defense attorney anyway? I would think you'd be glad to be rid of him. Especially him, judging by his reputation."

Brunelle wished he didn't think Ryder had a point. Not about never charging Beckle or Strunk being acquitted. About Welles. It was easy for Brunelle to fall into his default prosecutor mode and want to convict the defendant, but when he was reminded that the dead man was William Harrison Welles, he had to take the edge off his thirst for justice. Maybe Welles had met justice that night when he hit the floor of his office.

"We don't care if he was a criminal defense attorney," Carlisle answered for them. "We wouldn't even care if he worked at a fancy civil firm and took one criminal case so he could play pretend. Murder is murder."

"And justifiable homicide is justifiable homicide," Ryder rejoined, ignoring the swipe at him. "This is getting tedious. I understand that this hearing is required by the criminal court rules, but I believe we've reached the point where neither of is going to convince the other to change their position. Shall we fill out whatever order the judges require and begin our preparations for trial?"

Brunelle could hardly disagree with Ryder. But he wasn't going to give up trying to gain an advantage before the increasingly likely trial.

"Let us talk to Beckle," Brunelle said. "If he corroborates what Strunk said, we'll dismiss the case."

"What?" Carlisle's jaw dropped. "Are you joking? No, we won't." She looked at Ryder. "We won't dismiss the case. He's joking."

But Brunelle shook his head. "I'm not joking. I'm just being practical. Strunk and Beckle are the only witnesses, thanks to Welles being dead. If they say the same thing, we wouldn't be able to win the trial anyway. So, yeah, let's save ourselves some time. Make Beckle available. Let us question him. Let him confirm Strunk's story."

Ryder hesitated, considering Brunelle's proposal.

"Or shut up about Strunk being innocent and get ready for trial and hope the jury buys a bullshit story we can disprove with the crime scene photos."

Ryder remained silent for several more seconds. Finally he nodded slowly. "I will consider it."

Brunelle concealed his surprise. Ryder was definitely out of his element. He was going to make a mistake eventually trying to handle a criminal case. Brunelle just didn't expect it to be so soon, or so big. But he knew not to count his opponent's mistakes before they hatched.

"I can't ask for more than that," Brunelle said. It wasn't time for the hard sell.

"Yes, well, anyway." Ryder glanced around the room. "Where do they keep that pretrial order we need to fill out?"

Carlisle extracted one from her file. "Here. I already filled it out. I knew we wouldn't get anywhere."

Ryder accepted the document, then offered a grin to Brunelle. "Well, not yet anyway. Right, Mr. Brunelle?"

"Right, Mr. Ryder." Brunelle returned the grin and added a nod.

Carlisle rolled her eyes, but didn't say anything while Ryder signed the bottom of the form to confirm they had all been there and sort of tried to settle the case before moving forward toward trial. She took it into the courtroom to drop off for the judge to sign during a recess between the all-day calendar of guilty pleas. If you settled the case at the pretrial, you never had to leave The Pit. When she got back out, Ryder was gone.

"What the fuck was that?" she demanded. "You can't dismiss a murder case just because the defendant's best friend tells the same damn lie as the defendant."

"I know," Brunelle assured her.

Carlisle took a moment then shook her head. "But you just promised that. That is exactly what you promised."

"He won't do it," Brunelle dismissed Carlisle's concern. "It would be malpractice."

"It would be smart," Carlisle said. "I mean, without the promise to dismiss, yeah, sure, it's malpractice. But with the promise to dismiss? It's probably malpractice not to do it."

"He can't make me do it, Gwen," Brunelle hedged. "It's

not like it's a contract or something."

"Sounded like a contract to me, Dave," Carlisle replied. "But what do I know? I'm just a lawyer."

"Let's burn one bridge at a time." Brunelle tried to calm his partner down. "Before we have to worry about that, Ryder would have to decide to let Beckle talk to us, Beckle would have to agree to actually do it, and then he would have to say the same thing Strunk said. Even the smallest difference would let me wiggle out of whatever contract you and Ryder think I just made."

"Fire," Carlisle replied, pointing at Brunelle. "You. Playing with."

Brunelle shrugged. "I wasn't being flippant about the other part of this bargain—"

"Aha!" Carlisle jabbed a finger into Brunelle's chest. "It was a contract."

"Bargain," Brunelle insisted, although he knew there was no practical difference. "But seriously, if Beckle says the exact same thing Strunk said, we are in deep trouble. I'd sure like to know that now, and not in the middle of trial. Wouldn't you?"

Carlisle frowned and took a moment to answer. "I suppose."

Brunelle clapped her on the shoulder. "Sure you would. And so now either we will or we won't and it doesn't really matter because we have other stuff to do anyway."

Carlisle's brows lowered. "What things? I mean, I know there are a hundred things to do to prepare for a murder trial. But you seemed like you meant something specific."

"I did," Brunelle agreed. "And it's even more important if we're actually going to talk with Beckle. We need to dig into his past."

CHAPTER 8

Foster programs in Washington State were overseen by the Department of Social and Health Services. DSHS. DSHS also oversaw Western State Hospital, the state mental hospital which housed the criminally insane on the western side of the Cascade Mountains. The criminally insane on the other side of the mountains ended up at Eastern State Hospital. King County fed into Western State, so Brunelle had dealt with his fair share of defendants who had either started or ended their cases inside the walls of that underfunded mental institution.

But Brunelle hadn't delved into the part of DSHS that dealt with foster kids. To be sure, there were court proceedings that touched on that part of DSHS. He had never done them, but every Prosecutor's Office also had a team that handled dependencies, hearings where the State, through the local county prosecutor, was seeking to terminate someone's parental rights for the sake of the child or children involved. It was miserable work, immersing one's self into what the worst people did to the weakest. It made homicides seem like bedtime stories.

So, when Brunelle and Carlisle paid a visit to the DSHS

Office located just south of downtown, in what was still called the 'SoDo District' for being south of the Kingdome sport stadium—the dome that was demolished in 2000—the plan was to let DSHS think they were there to talk about a dependency case. They weren't going to lie, but they might try to pull another Ms. McFadden and let the DSHS employee think it was standard operating procedure to give them the information they wanted.

The SoDo District was a light industrial area slowly being rezoned into gentrified boutiques. While most of it was still one-story warehouses and semitruck parking lots, there were a few newer, trendier areas, featuring coffee houses and art galleries and other cool fun stuff. The DSHS Office wasn't located in any of those. It was in a building that was part one-story warehouse and part one-story office front. The parking lot was small and already full. Brunelle had to park up the street again.

"I want to be the bad cop," Carlisle said as they exited the car.

"This isn't good cop, bad cop," Brunelle replied. "It's good prosecutor and other good prosecutor."

"I bet that doesn't work," Carlisle predicted.

"If it doesn't, then you can be the bad cop," Brunelle offered.

"Fair enough," Carlisle agreed.

They had reached the entrance to the DSHS Office, and specifically the Home and Community Services Division. If there were any records of Beckle's stint in foster care—and of course there were—then that office would have them. Brunelle steeled himself to present a broad smile to the person at the receptionist desk and pulled the door open.

But there was no receptionist. There was a red 'take a number' dispenser on a stand immediately inside the door and a series of windows on the far wall, each of them either with a person already being helped or closed.

"Crap." Brunelle sighed. "This is going to take a while."

"And probably for nothing. A clerk at a window isn't going to give us confidential records."

Brunelle wanted to argue, but he suspected she was right. Still, he yanked a number ticket out of the dispenser. "Only one way to find out."

He looked at the ticket. "We are number 412."

They both looked up at the 'Now Serving' sign mounted above the row of windows. It read '388'. It was indeed going to take a while.

* * *

Eighty-seven minutes. That's how long Brunelle and Carlisle waited for the 'Now Serving' sign to climb from 388 to 412. The bad news was that he hadn't thought to bring any work with him. The good news was Carlisle had. Neither of them wanted to make small talk for eighty-seven minutes. They worked well together in trial. That didn't mean they were friends.

"Number four hundred and twelve!" called out the elderly gentleman at Window 6. 'Called out' might have been a generous description. He said the words, and he definitely tried to put some force behind them, but they were more of a louder wheeze than the man might normally offer in conversation. Regardless, they heard him and were both glad to finally get to try their 'good prosecutor/good prosecutor' schtick.

"Hello," Brunelle started. He was lead counsel after all. "My name is David Brunelle. This is Gwen Carlisle. We're with the King County Prosecutor's Office and we need to get a copy of some records for an upcoming case."

The man frowned. He was thin, with dry skin hanging

around his neck and thick lenses in frames that were at least two decades out of style. "You came to the front windows to get records?" he asked. "Why didn't you just call Gretchen? She's the one who usually gets the records together for the Prosecutor's Office."

"Gretchen," Brunelle turned to Carlisle, saying the name as if he should have realized.

"I told you to call Gretchen," Carlisle said, "but you just wouldn't listen to me, would you?"

Okay, thought Brunelle, maybe it was going to be good prosecutor/jerk prosecutor.

Carlisle rolled her eyes at Brunelle and looked at the man in the window. His nameplate said, 'Charles'.

"Charles, is it?" Gwen asked, gesturing toward the placard. She didn't wait for a response, although Charles offered a nod as she continued. "You've probably been around the block a bit, right? How long have you been at DSHS now?"

"Thirty-seven years next January," Charles was obviously proud to report.

"Thirty-seven years. Wow." Carlisle whistled appreciatively. "And in those thirty-seven years, how many times did you have some yahoo from another department transfer in and think he knew everything about everything already and had a hundred and one ideas for how to change things?"

Charles chuckled and nodded knowingly. "More times than I'd care to count," he reported.

"Exactly." Carlisle slapped the counter gently. She pointed to Brunelle. "See this guy here? This guy has been doing murder cases for the last decade or so and for some reason he thinks that makes him an expert in dependencies. Can you believe that?"

"Homicides?" Charles gasped. "Oh my."

"Oh yeah, super impressive," Carlisle agreed. "But that's precisely the problem. He's so used to everyone being impressed by him that he doesn't think to listen to the people who actually know how to get things done. 'Call Gretchen,' I say. But does he listen? No. And now here we are, sitting in the lobby for an hour and a half when we could have gotten the records we needed from Gretchen with one email."

"Gretchen hates email," Charles said. "She thinks it's rude. If you want to talk to her, then call her, she says. Don't leave her a note and expect her to drop everything when her in box chimes."

"Right. Yes. Gretchen hates email." Carlisle slapped the counter again. "I tried to tell him that too, but would he listen? Nooo."

"Could I say something?" Brunelle raised a finger.

"Go ahead, Mr. Know-It-All." Charles laughed, throwing a wink at Carlisle. "Are you going to tell me how to do my job too?"

Brunelle hesitated. He took a moment to remember that Carlisle wasn't actually criticizing him. It was an act. He needed to lean into it.

"Well, in the homicide division," Brunelle took on a professorial affect, "we always say, 'One person, one job'. Everyone needs to know their place. Ms. Carlisle here is still learning that, no matter how much she might think she knows about dependency cases. But here at DSHS, the same should be true. If Gretchen is indeed the person to contact, then you must not have the authorization to provide us with the information we need."

"I can get you the information as well as Gretchen can,"

Charles snapped back. "She's not special. We all have access to the records. She's just the one who sits at her desk all day waiting for the phone to ring while the rest of us work the counters."

"You can get us the records we need?" Carlisle enthused. "Really? That would be great."

"Sure I can," Charles answered. "What do you need?"

Brunelle pulled out a slip of paper with Beckle's full name and birthdate on it. He slid it across the counter. "We need the name and address of every foster family this individual lived with from the time he entered the foster care system."

Charles stared at the piece of paper, then looked at Carlisle again. "He really doesn't know how this works, does he?"

Carlisle chuckled and shook her head. "No, he really doesn't."

She doesn't either! Brunelle wanted to snap, but he stopped himself.

"Whatever information you can give us is great, Charles," Carlisle assured him. She patted Brunelle on the arm. "We can use this as a teaching moment."

Charles nodded in agreement, then turned to his computer terminal. "I can't just disclose every person who's ever fostered this, uh," he looked at the piece of paper, "Jonathan fellow. There are procedures for that kind of information. Court orders and what have you."

Brunelle wasn't going to seek a court order for the information. Filing a motion for a court order for release of all of Beckle's sensitive juvenile data would tip Ryder off that they were up to something. That was precisely why they had come to the lobby of the DSHS Office in SoDo.

"But what I can do," Charles went on, giving his temple a

tap, "is provide you with an address history. Everyone has an address history somewhere. Every time you get a speeding ticket, they enter it into the system and update your address."

"An address history?" Brunelle questioned.

"Yes, sir," Charles answered. "Every address we had for this fellow until he aged out of the system on his eighteenth birthday."

Carlisle raised an eyebrow at Brunelle and made the slier expression that warned, 'Do not screw this up.'

Brunelle smiled at the clerk. "Thanks, Charles. That'll be great. And I guess I've learned my lesson."

"And what lesson is that, young man?" Charles tested, even as the printer behind him began to whir.

"To call Gretchen," Brunelle answered proudly.

But Charles shook his head. "No, no," he scolded. He turned around, took the pages off the printer, and stapled them together.

"The real lesson," Charles explained as he handed the papers to Carlisle, "is to listen to this young woman right here. She's clearly the smart one."

CHAPTER 9

Smart prosecutor/dumb prosecutor. Carlisle was not going to let that one go, Brunelle knew. But the ruse had worked. They didn't have a full rundown of Jonathan Beckle's foster care history, but they had the addresses he'd lived at until he was eighteen. They could visit each address and hope the people living there were the same ones who had fostered young Jonathan as he grew up into the murderer Brunelle knew he was.

They decided to work backwards, believing that the most recent family would be the least likely to have moved away over the years and most likely to have salient information. How Little Jonny played with blocks when he was three wasn't going to be very useful. The most recent address was in Seattle, which meant minimal drive time. Brunelle had feared they might have to travel to remote corners of Washington to follow up on their lead. If an hour and a half at DSHS had been awkward, he wasn't looking forward to a four-hour road trip. Especially not when Carlisle would be armed with smart prosecutor/dumb prosecutor material.

It took a few days for Brunelle's and Carlisle's schedules

to line up again for a free afternoon to travel to the Columbia City neighborhood in South Seattle. It was another one of those areas that was gentrifying, but instead of brightening an industrial area, the new shops and boutiques were forcing their way into a traditionally lower income neighborhood and forcing out local residents and business owners. The fact that it had also been a traditionally minority neighborhood, thanks to generations of racism and redlining that occurred in Seattle just like everywhere else, made it even more sensitive. That was a larger conversation. But Brunelle was looking for a small one. One with the foster parents who had last sheltered Jonathan Beckle before he became an adult and had to make his own way in the world. One at 3516 S. Hudson Street.

It was a simple house. One of the typical three-bedroom ranch-style homes that had covered Seattle before all the tech money converted most of them into teardowns replaced with 3,000- square-foot mini-mansions. This one was still in its original condition, like all but one on that particular block. That one had opted for a faux stone veneer in earth tones and a circular driveway instead of a lawn. Brunelle thought it looked like an Olive Garden restaurant. But the one they were going to had wooden siding, painted a faded blue, and parking spot right out front. Finally.

"We are not," Brunelle declared preemptively, "playing smart prosecutor/dumb prosecutor."

Carlisle laughed. "You think we're not," she joked.

"Let's just play this one straight," Brunelle suggested. "Honest about who we are and why we're here and what kind of trouble Beckle is in."

"Or is not in," Carlisle pointed out, "but we want to put him in. Yeah, that should work great. 'Excuse me, sir or madam, do you recall that young man to whom you opened your home and hearts? Yes, we're trying to put him in prison for murder. Do you have a few minutes to help us?'"

Brunelle frowned, but she had a point. "Let's just refer to him as a witness and we're trying to get background. That's currently accurate. We don't need to get into our plans for his future."

"I can agree with that approach," Carlisle said.

She opened the gate in the chain-link fence surrounding the small property and ushered Brunelle through it. A moment later they were standing on a small cement porch. A moment after that, Brunelle knocked on the door.

Dogs began barking inside, followed shortly thereafter by a voice telling them all to shut the hell up. They did not, of course, and so when the woman who answered the door did so, she only opened it a few inches so as not to let out any of the noisemakers trying to push past her to see who had invaded their territory.

"Can I help you?" the woman asked. She seemed to be about 50, although she might have been younger with a scratchy voice from the chain-smoking that was obvious from the smell escaping through the cracked front door. She was heavyset, with graying hair pulled back into a ponytail, and wearing a sweatshirt and mismatched sweatpants. "You from the bank or something?"

Brunelle realized he and Carlisle were still in their court clothes. They probably looked like 'narcs' or whatever the kids were saying then for people who were uptight and worked for The Man. That is, people like prosecutors.

"No, ma'am," Brunelle answered. "We're from the King County Prosecutor's Office and we were hoping to talk with you about Jonathan Beckle."

Brunelle watched closely for any sign of recognition in the woman's face when he said Beckle's name. Even if she refused to speak with them, they would be able to tell if she was the foster parent—and not some new owner of the home—by the way her face reacted to hearing the name. A slight widening of the eyes or an exclamation stifled in her throat would be confirmation they had the right woman. But they didn't need any of that.

"Jonathan?! Oh, I remember Jonathan." Her face did react. It lit up happily. But then it dimmed slightly and she shook her head. "I knew he couldn't stay out of trouble. I hoped he would. But I knew he wouldn't."

That was news to Brunelle. Beckle's criminal history was clean. Like it had never happened.

"Do you have a few minutes to talk to us about Jonathan?" Carlisle asked. Friendly prosecutor.

"Of course, of course," the woman said. Then she looked down at the roiling mass of whining dogs at her feet, all still trying to get out. "Let's sit out back so these damn dogs don't jump all over your nice suits. You can just walk around. I'll meet you on the patio."

The patio was a cement slab with four plastic chairs, a plastic table, and an ashtray. There was also a small barbeque at the far edge, but its lid looked like it hadn't been opened in years. Brunelle brushed off one of the chairs and sat down carefully in it, lest his weight send it tumbling. Carlisle did the same and in a few moments they were joined by the woman of the house, who pushed through the rear sliding-glass door, deftly keeping her dogs inside with her foot.

"Sorry about them," she laughed. "They won't hurt you, but they will jump all over you. They should quiet down in a few minutes."

She made her way over to them and joined them around the small table and its ashtray. "You all mind if I smoke? I only smoke outside."

Brunelle didn't believe that, but he also didn't mind a person smoking in her own backyard. "Be our guest," he encouraged. "By the way, I'm Dave and this is Gwen. Like I said, we're—"

"From the Prosecutor's Office. Right." She finished his sentence. "I'm Maggie. I was Jonny's last foster mom before he turned eighteen and aged out."

"Do they get kicked out as soon as they turn eighteen?" Carlisle wondered.

Maggie shook her head as she lit her cigarette and pulled in the first drag of smoke. "Nah, we always let 'em stay for a little bit if they need it. But the checks stop coming, and there are other kids who need a place to stay. Jonny was a good kid. He had an apartment all set up and everything. I always liked him."

"How long was he with you?" Brunelle asked.

"Only about a year," Maggie recalled. "Maybe a year and a half. Long enough for Rich to straighten him out a bit before he had to start taking care of himself for real. Rich is my husband."

Brunelle had supposed as much. He was interested in a different part of her sentence. "Straighten him out?"

Maggie nodded, exhaling a plume of smoke out of her nose. "Yeah. These kids have it rough. Especially somebody like Jonny who'd grown up almost his whole life in the system. He was an orphan. Parents died in a house fire when he was five. No other family, so the State had to take care of him. He went to an orphanage first, and then into foster care. That's a long time to live without a family or a stable home. A kid is bound to get in trouble."

"You mentioned that before," Brunelle said. "Him getting into trouble."

Maggie nodded, but then had to cough a few times before she could say anything. "I'm guessing that's why you two are here. Prosecutors, right? So, he's gotten himself into trouble again, huh?"

Brunelle shrugged and looked at Carlisle. She returned the shrug.

"It's more like trouble is circling around him," she explained. "He was an eyewitness to a murder."

"A murder!" Another coughing attack. "Oh my! Oh, Jonny. What has he gotten himself into? And after all he did to get everything cleaned up. And now a murder? Was it someone he knew?"

Carlisle shook her head. "We don't think so. But the person who pulled the trigger was a friend of his. A young man about Jonny's same age. Name is Maximillian Strunk. Does that name ring any bells?"

Maggie thought for a moment, then shook her head as well. "No. I mean, I didn't know all of Jonny's friends. He was seventeen, you know? But I don't recall ever hearing the name Maximillian. I think I would have remembered that."

Likely, Brunelle thought. Also unlikely Jonny would have met the bad boy kid of a rich daddy while he was living in a foster home in South Seattle. They probably connected after Jonny moved north and started that new life Rich straightened him out for.

"So, did he get into a lot of trouble then, when he was with you?" Brunelle asked. "Is that why your husband had to straighten him out?"

Maggie pursed her lips slightly. "No, not when he was

with us. By then, I think he'd figured out he needed to stop getting in trouble so much. Or at least stop getting caught," she laughed. "But no, Rich just made it real clear what he expected of anyone living under our roof. That's always the first talk when a new kid arrives. We take in older kids, you know? The ones who are never gonna be adopted. The ones who are about to graduate from a system that barely cares about them into a world that definitely doesn't care about them. Rich is a good man. He works hard and he takes care of his own. So, when a new kid shows up, first thing Rich does is sit them down and explain expectations. You're gonna do this and you're not gonna do that and at the end you'll be as ready as you can be to go out and make your way."

She took a long drag of her cigarette, and relaxed into it without any coughing that time.

"Some people show their love with hugs and kisses, or with flowers and gifts. But Rich? Rich shows it the real way, the best way. He's a good man and he shows these young kids how to be good men too. That's the best thing you can ever do for a person. Those kids are lucky to have him." She smiled. "I'm lucky to have him."

Brunelle could see that was true. It sounded like Jonny had been lucky to have him too. Too bad he messed it all up.

"Do you happen to know who the family was where Jonny stayed before coming to your home?" he asked. It felt like they had gotten just about all of the information they needed from Maggie. They were ready to start daisy-chaining back in time.

But Maggie shook her head. "No, sorry, hon. They don't tell us that. I mean, they might if we needed to know, but we never needed to know. Once they walk in our front door, they're ours. It doesn't matter where they were before. It's better not to look back too much, if you know what I mean."

"Sure," Brunelle agreed.

"That's too bad," Carlisle put in. "We're trying to understand Jonny better. Trying to understand why he was there the night of the murder."

Maggie thought for a moment as she put her cigarette out in the ashtray. "The only thing I know about Jonny's past is the name of the orphanage he went to when his parents died. The Hutchinson School, they called it. Down in Aberdeen."

And there was the drive to a remote corner of Washington. Although not as remote as it could have been. Aberdeen was located about halfway up Washington's Pacific Coast, but it was still at least a two-hour drive from Seattle. Longer, if there was construction on Interstate-5. And there was always construction on Interstate-5.

"Thank you for your time, Maggie." Brunelle pushed himself out of his chair. "It was very helpful."

"I'm always here for my kids, Dave," Maggie said as she stood up too. Carlisle stood as well. "Even after they leave. Rich wouldn't like that, but I'm always a mama. Say hi to him for me, okay? Tell him Mama Maggie still thinks about him."

"I'm sure he'd love to hear that," Carlisle said.

Brunelle didn't say the other part: *But we're not allowed to talk to him.*

Or so they thought.

CHAPTER 10

Shortly after their visit to Mama Maggie, Brunelle found himself checking his schedule to see when he might be able to find time to drive to Aberdeen. Part of him was trying to find a time when he could definitely go and Carlisle probably couldn't. At best, the conversation would revolve around the case and the comparative merits of spending so much time and energy for a victim who probably deserved it and wouldn't be missed. At worst, it would be two to three hours of awkward silence. Even worse than that, Carlisle would pick the music. He knew he would hate it, no matter what it was. Everyone hated everyone else's music.

Fortunately—maybe—something more urgent came up. Brunelle read the email. Shook his head. Read it again. Then went down to Carlisle's office to tell her.

"You are not going to believe this," he said.

"I bet I will," Carlisle looked up from her desk. "Ryder called your bluff. He's going to make Beckle available for an interview."

Brunelle surrendered a half-grin. "How did you know

that? Were you guessing or did you just figure he would because I'm the dumb prosecutor and you're the smart prosecutor?"

"I was cc'd on the email, Dave," Carlisle pointed out. "I 'll let you deduce who's the dumb prosecutor."

"Oh," Brunelle replied. "I guess I didn't notice that. But can you believe it? The attorney is going to let us interrogate his client about the murder he committed."

"The attorney," Carlisle crossed her arms, "is going to let his client tell us someone else committed the murder so we have to dismiss the case against his other client. I'm not as excited about this as you are."

That much was obvious. "Well, I'm not as pessimistic about this as you are. He's going to say something different. Guaranteed. Even if he wanted to say the exact same thing as Strunk, he'll leave something out. We'll make sure of it."

"How are you going to do that?" Carlisle scoffed. "You're no detective. Your interrogations are in front of a jury with a judge making sure everybody plays fair."

"Which is exactly why we're going to have Chen do the questioning."

* * *

"Wait. What?" Brunelle couldn't see Chen's face over the phone, but he could imagine his expression. "The lawyer who represents Strunk also represents Beckle and he's going to let me take another run at Beckle?"

"That's right." Brunelle grinned up at Carlisle, who was listening in on the call over speakerphone.

"Why would he do that?" Chen asked.

"Because Dave promised to dismiss the case against both of them afterward," Carlisle called out.

"What? Are you crazy? Why would you do that?"

"That's not exactly what I said," Brunelle frowned at his co-counsel. "I said, if Beckle says the exact same thing as Strunk, then that would probably torpedo our case anyway."

"That's not what he said, Larry," Carlisle put in. "He promised to dismiss it."

"If Beckle says the exact same thing as Strunk," Brunelle defended, "which he won't."

"Of course he will," Chen said. "That lawyer will give him a copy of what Strunk said and have him memorize it word for word. Hell, what do you even need me for?"

"I need you to make sure he doesn't do that," Brunelle explained.

"How am I going to do that?" Chen asked, clearly exasperated.

"Here's how," Brunelle grinned, and he proceeded to lay out his plan.

* * *

Brunelle reached out and shook Ryder's hand as the lawyer and his not-charged (yet) client arrived at the King County Prosecutor's Office for the interview they had both agreed to. "Thanks for coming, Mr. Ryder."

"Thank you for the suggestion, Mr. Brunelle," Ryder replied. "I'm certain this will be productive and lead to a favorable resolution for both of my clients."

Brunelle withheld comment on that. Instead, he thanked the receptionist for escorting his guests to the conference room and stepped aside to gesture at its occupants. "I think you know everyone already. My co-counsel, Ms. Carlisle. And Detective Larry Chen. You may not know him yet, but your client certainly does. Or rather, both of your clients know him."

Brunelle looked at Beckle, standing tentatively behind his

attorney. His expression confirmed he hadn't forgotten Chen or his time, however brief, in police custody.

"Nice to meet you, Detective Chen." Ryder nodded to him. If he had any concerns about the police doing the questioning instead of a prosecutor, he didn't let it show. "Shall we get started? I'm sure we all have other things to do and I'm eager to get to the result of this very worthwhile endeavor."

I'm sure you are, Brunelle thought. He had shown bravado in front of Carlisle and Chen, but he was actually a little disconcerted about the entire thing. Ryder was too confident, too friendly. He knew what his client was going to say, and it was going to be identical to the transcript of what his other client said.

They all took seats around the conference table. Brunelle and Carlisle sat on one side, Ryder and Beckle on the other, and Chen between them at the head of the table. He placed a recorder between them all and pressed 'Record'".

"This is Detective Larry Chen of the Seattle Police Department," he began the recording with a recitation of the parties present, the date and time, and the fact that everyone present had consented to the recording, to confirm no one was violating Washington's rather strict laws regarding recording private communications. Then, he looked to Ryder. "Are we ready to begin?"

Ryder looked to his client. "Ready, Jonathan?"

Beckle didn't appear particularly ready. But he trusted his lawyer. "Yes," he croaked.

Ryder turned back to Chen and nodded. "We're ready, Detective. You may begin."

All very formal and somehow theatrical. Brunelle had several reasons why he didn't want to see the case dismissed, but one of those was definitely curiosity about how Ryder would comport himself in front of a jury. Brunelle expected he'd acquit himself quite well. Just so long as he didn't acquit Strunk too.

"Mr. Beckle," Chen leaned forward slightly and crossed his hands on the tabletop, "please tell us why you went to see Mr. Welles that evening. Did it have something to do with troubles during your stay in foster care as a juvenile?"

"Whoa!" Ryder threw his hands up. "Objection."

Brunelle frowned at his opponent. "This isn't a courtroom, Ryder. There's no judge here. You don't need to say, 'Objection'. That doesn't even make sense."

"I can object to something without being in court, Brunelle," Ryder huffed. "And I certainly do object to questioning about my client's youthful past. This is about what happened that night. That was the deal. You ask him what happened, and if he says the same thing as Mr. Strunk—which he will—then you dismiss."

Brunelle shrugged slightly. "I'm not sure that's exactly the deal. The deal was that we get to question him about the incident, and I agreed that if his story supported Strunk's statement, then I would be hard pressed to continue the prosecution."

"That's just a lot of slippery lawyer words." Ryder wagged his finger at Brunelle. "Are you trying to back out of our deal now? Is that why you're not even asking about what happened? To avoid the deal?"

"I think we can agree what happened that night begins with why they were there in the first place," Brunelle replied. "We'll get to how and why they shot and killed Mr. Welles, but first I want to know why they were there. None of it makes sense if I don't know that."

But Ryder wasn't having it. He shook his head vigorously. "You are not asking about my client's prior history. It's irrelevant and it's off limits."

Brunelle nodded thoughtfully. He'd hit a nerve. That was good. That meant there was something there. They were going to keep digging. He'd hoped Chen could start the mining, but there were other shafts to explore.

"Okay." Brunelle threw his hands up. "I guess we're done. Thanks for coming. I guess we'll see you in court. Literally."

"Wait. That's it?" Ryder demanded. "You're not even going to let him make a statement about the incident?"

Chen looked to Brunelle. Brunelle nodded to him. And Chen turned off the recorder.

"Nope," Brunelle answered. "I never expected him to tell the truth about what happened. I was just hoping he might help us understand why it happened."

Ryder's face flushed. He jabbed a finger at Chen. "Turn that recorder back on! I will make an offer of proof as to what my client would have said had he been allowed to."

"You're demanding your client confess to the police?" Carlisle questioned. "Are you sure you know how to do a criminal case? That's not really standard operating procedure."

Chen looked to Brunelle. Brunelle shook his head. Chen didn't turn the recorder back on.

"Really?" Ryder's eyes darted between his opponents. "That's how you're playing this? Well, fine. No, that's fine." He slammed himself to his feet. Beckle followed tentatively. "There are other ways to establish what Mr. Beckle would have said. He was prepared to meet his part of the agreement, and he is entitled to the benefit of the bargain."

Ryder stormed out of the conference room, client in tow.

"Think he can find his way out?" Carlisle asked.

Brunelle shrugged. "Probably. Rachel will find him if he makes enough noise, which seems likely."

"So, I don't know: did that go well?" Chen asked.

"It went about how I expected," Brunelle answered. "Although I was hopeful Ryder would let him answer at least one question."

"I found it entertaining," Carlisle put in. "So, that's a win. And we know there's something there when it comes to Beckle's troubled youth."

"But no criminal history," Brunelle recalled, with a frown.

"Maybe administrative proceedings within the foster system?" Carlisle suggested. "If that's even a thing."

Brunelle shrugged. "Might be. But we'd need to know what county. We can do a search here in King County easy enough. Our offices are literally inside the courthouse."

"But we don't know if he's been in King County the whole time," Carlisle knew.

"Where else would he have been?" Chen asked.

"He finished his childhood in Seattle," Brunelle answered, "but it started in Aberdeen. Grays Harbor County."

Carlisle threw her hands up. "Road trip!" she laughed. "I get to choose the music."

CHAPTER 11

Two hours, forty-seven minutes. That was how long the drive from Seattle to Aberdeen took. It should have been shorter, but there was construction and a lane closure by the Tacoma Dome and traffic always slowed down going through Joint Base Lewis McChord, the Army and Air Force installation between Tacoma and Olympia. After that it was pretty clear sailing—or driving, rather—and Brunelle was pleasantly surprised to find that he didn't completely hate Carlisle's taste in music.

Still, it was a long drive. Avoiding small talk was impossible. But then they stumbled on the most entertaining form of small talk: gossip. They say don't speak ill of the dead, but when you're a prosecutor, it's just trial prep.

"You think we'll end up missing Welles?" Carlisle asked. "Or just forget about him? He seems pretty unforgettable. I always hated that jackass."

Brunelle considered for a moment. "I don't think I'll forget him exactly, but I'm not going to miss him either."

Carlisle nodded. "I'm not surprised he met a violent end. Some of those private defense attorneys, they're just making a living, you know? They know their clients suck, but it's a job; it pays the bills. And the public defenders—the lifers, I mean—they think their clients are saints, or persecuted victims in need of rescue. But Welles? It was like he was one of them, you know? He just happened to be the one with the bar card."

"That's probably why Beckle went to him," Brunelle hypothesized. "His reputation preceded him."

Carlisle nodded. "Good theory. Welles definitely had a reputation. I mean, if I were ever in serious trouble, I would have hired him. He was a jackass, but he was good. Didn't he beat you a few times?"

Brunelle grimaced. "We don't need to talk about that. But yes, he was good. One of the best."

"That means Beckle thought he needed the best," Carlisle deduced. "But why? Was he planning something?"

"Trying to get legal advice in advance about how to commit a crime and get away with it?" Brunelle considered. "I guess that might make sense. A lot of attorneys wouldn't take that case, but Welles would. As long as he got paid."

"Okay, so now we have a working theory," Carlisle nodded. "They went to Welles to get legal advice on a crime they were planning."

"I like that," Brunelle said.

"Oh my God!" Carlisle almost shouted. "What if the crime they were planning was murdering Welles? That would be so fucked up."

"Wow," Brunelle considered. "Mr. Lawyer, how would we get away with murdering someone? Use self-defense or defense of others, and make sure you have a witness on your side but none on the other side. Cool, thanks, *blam blam blam*!"

"Exactly!" Carlisle nearly shouted.

"That is fucked up," Brunelle agreed. "We can't argue that."

"I mean, not without evidence," Carlisle agreed. "But I'm keeping that in my back pocket in case we don't get anything better."

"You know we don't have to prove motive, right?" Brunelle pointed out the law on the subject.

"You know the jury is going to want us to anyway, right?" Carlisle pointed out the truth on the subject.

"Yeah," Brunelle sighed. "I'm just worried we're never going to figure it out. Welles may have been a dirty jackass who no one on our side is going to miss, but we can't exactly say that to the jury, can we? We need more. We need to know why Jonathan Beckle thought he needed a lawyer that night."

Carlisle pointed to the large institutional building looming through the windshield. "Then let's hope we begin to find our answer within the surprisingly ominous walls of Hutchinson House."

They had arrived at their destination.

* * *

There was ample parking in front of the enormous orphanage where five-year-old Jonathan Beckle was delivered after the tragic death of both of his parents. Pillars and gables covered the façade and roof. A pair of large wooden doors stood above a dozen cement steps and under a stone-carved sign that read, 'HUTCHINSON HOUSE, HOME FOR CHILDREN'.

Brunelle stood at the bottom of the stairs and looked up at the imposing entrance. He took a moment to acknowledge how much tragedy and terribleness filled his day-to-day life, albeit from a professional distance. Then he made himself forget again and started up the steps. He had a job to do.

The interior of Hutchinson House was as grand as its exterior. The main lobby was palatial, with a ceiling that reached the top of the second story and a sweeping staircase that led up to what Brunelle guessed were the residential quarters. The décor was dark wood and white walls, with framed artwork on all the walls and comfortable chairs tucked off to the side. It would have been a lovely place to live, but for the entrance requirements.

On the far left of the lobby was a front desk, made of the same darkly finished wood. A young woman with long red hair and a dark sweater was seated behind the desk, reading a book. She looked up when Brunelle and Carlisle entered.

"Hello," she called out, a slight echo bouncing off the cavernous entry. "Welcome to Hutchinson House."

Brunelle smiled and nodded. "Thank you."

"How can we help you?" the woman asked.

Brunelle and Carlisle made their way over toward the desk.

"We were hoping to ask someone," Carlisle explained, "about a young boy who came here after his parents died in a house fire, probably about sixteen or seventeen years ago."

The young woman nodded. "Of course," she seemed to agree without really agreeing. "Are you family of this young boy perhaps?"

"Not exactly," Brunelle hedged.

"Not at all," Carlisle corrected. It looked like it was going to be disingenuous prosecutor/honest prosecutor. "We're from the King County Prosecutor's Office. In Seattle."

"I know where King County is, ma'am." The woman smiled. "And you've come all the way down here to ask about this child. It must be important."

"It is," Brunelle confirmed. "It pertains to a murder

investigation. We believe you may have information that could be vital to solving the case and holding the killers responsible."

"Information about a boy from seventeen years ago could do that?" the redheaded woman asked. "Well, that does sound important. Let me get the director. I'm sure she would want to be the one to talk to you about this."

Brunelle expressed his thanks and turned to Carlisle as the woman disappeared down the hallway behind the front desk.

"Do you think they'll tell us anything?" he asked.

Carlisle nodded. "I think so. This is a private institution. They can make their own rules about what information to provide. We just need to sell it."

Like with a jury, Brunelle thought. He hadn't realized when he went to law school that he was actually going into sales. Except, instead of hawking widgets, he was a salesman of something far more ethereal. Justice. Or at least the version of justice he was peddling.

"Hello!" a tall woman with long wavy gray hair and half glasses perched on her pointed nose announced as she emerged from the hallway, the young redheaded woman behind her. "I'm Victoria Blackwell, the Director of Hutchinson House. Stephanie tells me you have some questions about one of our children from some time ago. Something to do with a murder up in Seattle?"

"That's it exactly," Brunelle confirmed. "Would you have a few moments to speak with us? It really is very important."

"Of course, of course," Blackwell answered. She gestured back down the hall from whence she came, even as Stephanie retook her perch behind the front desk. "Let's go back to my office. It's a bit cozier than this overly large lobby."

"I like the lobby," Brunelle commented, glancing around again. "It seems important and welcoming all at once."

Blackwell smiled. "That is the goal. After all, the children who enter here are at the lowest point in their lives. We can't change what's brought them to us, but we want them to feel important, and welcomed. And loved."

They followed Blackwell down the hallway to her office, a large affair with floor-to-ceiling windows facing an interior courtyard and books strewn about on just about every surface. Rather than sit behind her leather-topped desk, Blackwell directed her guests to a circle of chairs around a coffee table near the windows. It reminded Brunelle of a similar furniture arrangement in Welles's office.

"Can I offer you some tea?" Blackwell picked up a teapot that had been resting on the table. "It's still warm."

Brunelle demurred. "No, thank you."

"I'll take some," Carlisle accepted. "It was a long drive. I could use a little pick-me-up."

Again, honest prosecutor. Brunelle was trying to be polite, which could be a form of disingenuousness. "Well, I guess maybe I'll have a cup after all," he admitted. "It was a long drive."

A few minutes later each of them was cradling a cup of warm tea.

"Now then," Blackwell began, "how can I help you?"

Brunelle looked to Carlisle, who gestured back at him to do the talking. It was his case after all. Senior prosecutor/junior prosecutor.

"Gwen and I are prosecuting a murder case up in Seattle," he recounted. "There are two people who were involved in the murder. Three if you count the victim. One of them pulled the trigger, but the other one appears to have been the one whose idea it was to go see the victim that night. And we're trying to figure out why."

"He didn't tell you?" Blackwell asked.

"He invoked his right to remain silent," Carlisle explained.

"Ah." Blackwell took a sip of her tea. "That was probably the smart thing to do."

Brunelle frowned slightly. "Probably, but it left us wondering what the motive for the shooting was. We decided to do a little digging about the non-shooter, a young man named Jonathan Beckle."

Brunelle took a beat to gauge Blackwell's reaction to the name. If she had one, it was imperceptible. Either she really didn't recognize the name, or she knew not to show it to two strangers suddenly appearing on her doorstep like, well, a couple of orphans.

"We discovered that he had been in the foster care system, so we contacted DSHS," Carlisle explained. "Then we spoke with his last foster family, and—"

"DSHS told you who his foster family was?" Blackwell interrupted. She was obviously dismayed.

"Not exactly," Brunelle assured. "We were able to obtain a last known address, so we went out there, and the woman who lived there was kind enough to talk with us, not unlike yourself. She confirmed she was Jonathan's foster mother when he turned eighteen."

"She was the one who told us that Jonathan had come here as an orphan when he was about five," Carlisle added, "after his parents died in a fire."

Blackwell nodded a bit and took another sip of tea. Brunelle couldn't tell if the nod meant that she understood what Mama Maggie had done, or that Jonathan had indeed come to Hutchinson House when he was five, or that she wasn't going to confirm or deny anything so she would just nod along.

"How would the young man having come here as a boy of five," Blackwell asked, "have any bearing whatsoever on why he would be involved in a murder some two decades later? Do you think someone who grows up in such difficulties must naturally turn to a life of crime? If so, I must say, I find that very disappointing."

Brunelle raised his hands defensively. "Oh, no. Nothing like that," he assured. "Just the contrary. It appears that he grew up, stayed out of the court system, and ended up with a good job in Seattle. That's why we're looking for answers. In some ways, it would make a lot more sense if he had turned to a life of crime, if this had been a robbery gone wrong instead of two young men murdering William Harrison Welles, one of Seattle's most famous criminal defense attorneys."

"Infamous," Carlisle suggested.

Brunelle considered then agreed. "Yes, infamous."

Blackwell didn't say anything for a few moments. Her expression had shifted, although to what Brunelle wasn't quite sure. She set her cup down on the table.

"Did you say the man who was murdered was William Welles?" she asked. "Billy Welles?"

"Uh…" Brunelle looked over at Carlisle who returned his confused expression. "I've never heard anyone call him Billy, but yes, the murder victim was William Harrison Welles, a local attorney. I actually had several cases against him during his career. We both did."

Blackwell's smile returned, albeit weaker and softer than before. "I'm sure you did. Billy made quite a success of himself. That's why we make sure they feel important, welcomed, and loved."

Brunelle had to take a moment to allow two plus two to equal four. "Wait." he raised a questioning hand. "Are you saying William Welles was an orphan here too?"

Blackwell nodded. "Oh yes. He lived here for over a year after his mother passed away from cancer. His father had died some years before. He was a wonderful little boy, an absolute spark. He helped the staff however he could and always looked out for the younger children. In the short time he was here, he made Hutchinson House a better place to live. And after he left, and became the successful man you just described, he continued to make Hutchinson House a better place to live. We will miss his support greatly, I'm afraid."

"Support?" Carlisle asked. "He donated to your facility?"

Blackwell smiled broadly. "It was far more than a donation. He helped us set up a series of financial accounts, and funded them, to ensure we would thrive in our mission should the day ever come that he could no longer help us. And it appears that day has come."

Brunelle looked disbelievingly at Carlisle. She mirrored his shock.

"Not just that," Blackwell added. "He also helped the children. If any of them needed legal help, either while they were here or afterward, he always made himself available, and at no charge."

Blackwell shook her head and blinked back a tear as she turned to gaze out at the courtyard. "I should have liked to thank him one more time."

Brunelle was absolutely speechless. Carlisle also had nothing to say. But they were lawyers, so after a moment, they forced themselves to talk. And since they were lawyers, they naturally focused on their own interests.

"Um, so, are you able to confirm that Jonathan Beckle was an orphan here?" Brunelle asked.

"And could you tell us where he went when he left to go into foster care?" Carlisle added.

Blackwell turned back slowly from the window. She smiled warmly and nodded. "No. I can't tell you any of that. But I am grateful for the news you brought me, if only to know the truth sooner. Poor, poor Billy. He was a good man."

* * *

"Bullshit. He was not a good man." Brunelle stomped down the front steps toward his car. "There is no way William Harrison Welles—"

"Billy Welles," Carlisle interjected with a chuckle.

Brunelle shook his head. "He was not a good man who donated money to orphans. I refuse to believe that."

"I don't know," Carlisle considered. "The jury might like that better than 'scumbag defense attorney'. Suddenly, we have a sympathetic victim. Young orphan boy grows up to be a successful attorney, pours largesse on those who helped him in his youth, only to be gunned down by two ruthless thugs for no reason. A pillar of the community, stricken down in his prime."

They had reached the bottom of the steps. Brunelle stopped and sighed. "That does sound better." He shook his head. "I can't believe I'm going to have to say nice things about William Harrison Welles."

"Billy Welles," Carlisle corrected again. "I think we should run with that. Everyone can imagine hating a pompous ass who calls himself by three names, but little Billy Welles? Why would anyone ever want to hurt sweet little Billy Welles?"

"You're right." Brunelle put a hand to his chin. "That is the question. Why did Beckle want to hurt him?"

"What about Strunk?" Carlisle asked. "He's the one who pulled the trigger."

"No." Brunelle frowned and shook his head. "Strunk lied through his teeth during most of that interrogation, but there's one thing I do believe. It was Beckle's idea to go there, and Strunk wasn't even paying attention until Welles reacted to whatever Beckle said to him."

"This has to be connected," Carlisle gestured back up the stairs. "You heard Blackwell. Welles would help people who were orphans here. Maybe he tried to help Beckle and screwed it up."

"Or maybe Beckle asked for help, expecting to get it," Brunelle posited, "and Welles said no."

Brunelle sighed and took a moment to gather his thoughts. He rubbed a hand over his head and looked at the time. It was almost 5:00. The Grays Harbor County Courthouse would close before they got there, and there was no way he was driving all the way back down there a second time.

"Let's find a place to eat," he suggested, "and figure out where we're staying tonight."

"Staying tonight?" Carlisle gasped. "I'm ready to head back up north."

"Me too," Brunelle consoled, "but I've got a feeling that the answers we need are hidden down here."

CHAPTER 12

The Grays Harbor Courthouse was in the city of Montesano, which was actually a few miles closer to Seattle than Aberdeen. Brunelle and Carlisle spent the night at a nondescript hotel in Aberdeen. Clean enough, and pretty cheap, being relatively far away from the state's larger cities to the north. The hotel didn't serve breakfast, but there was a Starbucks on the way out of town. Carlisle ran in to get the drinks while Brunelle stayed in the car and called his paralegal to let her know he and Carlisle wouldn't be in the office that morning.

"Good morning," came the voice of Nicole Richards, the lead paralegal in the homicide unit. "This is Nicole."

"Hey, Nicole. It's Dave," he said. "I'm just calling to check in. Carlisle and I are down in Aberdeen following up a lead on the Strunk case."

"Aberdeen?"

"Well, soon to be Montesano," Brunelle clarified. "That's where the courthouse is. Long story."

"I bet," Nicole laughed. "So, do you think you'll be in the office at all today?"

Brunelle thought for a moment. He didn't know how long they were going to need at the courthouse, but he did know unless they left well before lunch, they would hit Olympia and then Tacoma at rush hour, and there would be no way they could get to Seattle before 5:00.

"Eh, probably not," Brunelle admitted. "Not the way traffic is on I-5 in the afternoon."

"Okay, well, then hold on," Nicole said. "I just put something on your desk. I don't think you're going to want to wait until tomorrow to see it."

"What is it?" Brunelle asked, a knot twisting in his stomach.

"Just hold on," Nicole repeated. "I'll read it to you verbatim."

"That bad, huh?" Brunelle joked.

"Actually, yes," Nicole answered. "Be right back."

That knot in his stomach formed fully. Nicole was a highly competent professional with a calm, confident demeanor. If she thought something couldn't wait one day, then it probably was that bad.

"Okay, you still there?" Nicole asked when she got back on the line.

"I'm hardly going to hang up with that intro," Brunelle answered. "You've got me a little nervous."

"Oh good," Nicole said. "It'll be a short trip from that to scared."

Scared?" Brunelle asked.

"Panicked?" Nicole suggested.

"I don't panic," Brunelle insisted.

Nicole chuckled at that. "Sure, Dave. I've seen you in trial when everything is crumbling around you. You manage to pull it all together in the end usually, but it's not for lack of panic."

Brunelle didn't like the thought of other people observing his very observable traits. "Just read whatever it is. Which case is it on?" Although he was pretty sure he knew.

"Oh, it's the Strunk case," Nicole confirmed. "Okay, you ready?"

"I was born ready."

"Seriously, Dave. Stop," Nicole admonished. "This is serious."

Brunelle could tell. That's why he was deflecting with attempts at humor. "Okay. Go ahead. What does it say?"

"State of Washington versus Maximillian Strunk," Nicole read the caption first. "Defendant's motion to dismiss."

"They always file a motion to dismiss," Brunelle tried to sound unconcerned.

"I'm not done," Nicole said. "Defendant's motion to dismiss. Defendant's motion for specific performance."

"Specific performance?" Brunelle interrupted. "That's a contract law concept."

"Again, not done, Dave," Nicole chided. "Motion for specific performance. Motion to enforce criminal plea agreement."

"Plea bargain?" Brunelle asked.

"Did you really agree to dismiss the case, Dave?" Nicole asked. "That's what he's saying. He's asking the judge to enforce your promise to dismiss the case."

Damn it, Brunelle thought.

"No," Brunelle assured her. "I mean, kinda, but not really."

"Seriously, Dave? What does that mean?"

"It means," Brunelle explained, "that I said I would

probably have to dismiss the case if— You know what, never mind. It's complicated. I didn't agree to dismiss the case. And even if I did, he didn't live up to his side of the bargain, so I'm off the hook."

"I don't know, Dave," Nicole warned. "This motion is like twenty pages thick. I skimmed it and there's a lot of stuff in there. He says you had an enforceable agreement. He says he and his client acted in good faith to comply with it. He says you acted in bad faith to frustrate it. He says he's entitled to the benefit of the bargain he struck with you. And he cites a lot of cases, Dave. A lot."

"I can cite cases, too," Brunelle insisted.

"Cases about enforcement of contracts?" Nicole challenged. "You've never done a contracts case, Dave. That's civil, and you've been doing criminal since you graduated from law school."

That was true enough. One thing he liked about Nicole, among many, was that she was always honest with him, even if it might seem unkind. Brunelle was done arguing whether there was any merit to Ryder's motion.

"He scheduled it for oral argument, too, didn't he?" Brunelle knew the answer.

"He sure did."

"When?

"One week from today."

Five court days. That was the minimum notice you had to give opposing counsel for a hearing on any motion you filed. And why would you ever give more notice than the minimum?

"Okay, thanks, Nicole." Brunelle spied Carlisle returning, a grande in each hand. "Go ahead and leave it on my desk after all. I'll swing by the office before I go home, even if it's after hours."

"Sounds good, Dave," Nicole said. "Sorry to be the bearer of bad news."

Brunelle smiled a lopsided smile. "Bad news is the only news we deal with."

Nicole agreed and they ended the call just as Carlisle dropped into the car and handed Brunelle his coffee.

"Who was that?" she asked.

"Oh, uh. Nicole," Brunelle answered. "Ready to go to beautiful downtown Montesano?"

"Is everything okay?" Carlisle asked, her brow creasing.

"Oh, yeah, sure," Brunelle assured. "Nothing to worry about."

Carlisle waited a moment, then laughed. "Are you fucking kidding me, Brunelle? This is my case too. We're partners. I'm not your wife and you just got bad news from the bank about your loan application. You don't get to keep bad news from me like I need protecting. If shit hits the fan, you tell me. Period."

Brunelle listened, then relented. "Ryder filed a motion to dismiss, demanding specific performance of my promise to dismiss the case if Beckle spoke to us. He's citing a bunch of contract law doctrines, saying I acted in bad faith and demanding the benefit of the bargain."

Carlisle took a moment to consider. "Shit, that's good," she admired. "You're in trouble."

"I thought we were partners?" Brunelle complained.

"Depends." Carlisle took a sip of her coffee. "If we lose at trial, we lose together. But if you lose this motion, Dave, you lose alone."

* * *

The Grays Harbor County Courthouse was a stately stone structure topped by a clock tower dome. It looked like a smaller version of a lot of state capitol buildings. Rather than legislators and their aides, it housed courtrooms and the county clerk. As interesting as it might have been to peek at the courtrooms in another county, the Clerk's Office was their destination. It didn't matter what was happening in the courthouse that day; what mattered was what had happened in the past.

"So, what's the plan?" Carlisle asked as they entered the depository of all the county's official records, including court records. "Are we looking for cases with Beckle's name on them or with Welles's name? Or both?"

"Both would be good," Brunelle answered, "but maybe unlikely. I'm not sure really. I think anything involving either of them would be useful. Or maybe not. For all I know, Welles started practicing down here before he moved up to Seattle and became a big shot. There might be hundreds of cases where he defended local shoplifters or trespassers."

"So, let's start with Beckle," Carlisle reasoned. "His last foster mom said he'd gotten into trouble as a youth. Maybe there's something here to support that."

Brunelle frowned. "Maybe, but I wouldn't think so. His criminal history is clear. No convictions. Not even cases that were filed but ultimately dismissed. It's perfectly clean."

"Which is suspicious, if you ask me," Carlisle said. "I'd expect to see at least an MIP or something."

The court records had largely been converted from paper to digital and so they were able to search the database for cases that might include Beckle as a party, perhaps as a juvenile defendant, or maybe a petitioner trying to seal records, or the child of interest in a dependency or adoption or other family law proceeding.

"Nothing," Carlisle announced, looking up from one of the public computer terminals. "There's nothing in here with the name Jonathan Beckle."

Brunelle was seated at the terminal next to her. He hadn't found anything either, and they hadn't hurried. They wanted to be thorough but after what was starting to feel like far too much time, they weren't any closer to information about Jonathan Beckle than they were when they left Hutchinson House the previous day.

He rubbed the back of his neck. "Let's try Welles now. Even if we can't connect him to Beckle somehow, we might learn more about our victim. That's never a bad thing."

Carlisle shook her head and chuckled darkly. "That sounds like what someone says when they know they're about to fail at their primary task."

"It's always good to have secondary tasks," Brunelle counseled. "Otherwise, this job would be unbearable."

It already was sometimes, Brunelle thought to himself. Their mission at the Grays Harbor County Courthouse was shaping up to be a disappointment, and the only thing he had to look forward to on the other side of it was drafting the response to Ryder's motion to dismiss for Brunelle's mistake. Alleged mistake, he supposed. But alleged pretty hard. His stomach tightened again, so he shook the thoughts of tomorrow from his head and zeroed in on today's task. Another coping mechanism to keep the job from becoming unbearable.

Small successes also helped. Just enough encouragement to keep running the race.

"I think I found something," Carlisle announced. "He definitely used to practice down here when he started. I found a bunch of throw away garbage misdemeanors he was the defense attorney on. But then he stops appearing on any cases at all."

"When he moved to Seattle," Brunelle surmised.

"Probably," Carlisle agreed. "So, you'd think that would be the last you'd see of him down here, but then a few years later, he starts showing up here and there on older cases, filing motions to vacate convictions."

Brunelle frowned. "I've always hated that people can get their old convictions vacated if they just go long enough without a new charge. I mean, what's the point of prosecuting them if they can convert a conviction to a dismissal ten years later?"

"Agreed," Carlisle said. "But we don't draft the laws. I guess the Legislature wants to encourage people to rehabilitate or something."

"Pfft, fools," Brunelle half-joked.

"Right?" Carlisle agreed. "But anyway, yeah, it looks like he started doing that for people. It's kind of random. I wonder if there's some connection between these people."

Brunelle considered the other reason Welles kept a legal hand down south. "Maybe they're alumni of Hutchinson House too?"

"Alumni?" Carlisle laughed. "It's an orphanage, not a school, Dave."

"Whatever. You know what I mean. We should cross-reference the names."

"Good luck with that," Carlisle said. "I doubt Lady Blackwell will confirm any particular person was ever a resident there."

Brunelle cocked his head at her. "Lady Blackwell?"

Carlisle shrugged. "Feels like it fits. It fits, right?"

"Yeah, it kind of does," Brunelle admitted. "And yeah,

you're right. She won't help us. Maybe Charles at DSHS?"

But Carlisle shook her head. "We have to be careful not to get lost down a rabbit hole. We still haven't connected Beckle to Welles, and now we have that motion to dismiss to deal with. That kind of needs to be our priority, honestly."

Brunelle could hardly disagree. He glanced at the clock. It was approaching noon already, and they had a long drive ahead of them.

"Okay, let's spend fifteen more minutes," he said. "See if we find anything else. Then we hit the road."

"We hit Starbucks, then the road," Carlisle countered.

"Deal."

It was fourteen minutes later that Brunelle found something he thought might be significant. He thought it might be significant because he couldn't figure out what it was. And that was the exact opposite of what keeping records was supposed to accomplish.

"I found something," he said, "I think."

"You think?" Carlisle leaned over to look at his computer. "What does that mean?"

Brunelle pointed at his screen. "Look at that list of case entries. They have Welles as the attorney, but no parties listed. No other information at all. Just a case number and attorney of record. I can't even tell what kind of case it was or what he filed, if anything."

"He must have filed something," Carlisle supposed, "or his name wouldn't be on it."

"These aren't that old," Brunelle observed. "Five cases, all between ten and three years ago."

"When Beckle would have been a teenager," Carlisle did the math.

"When he would be most likely to get into trouble," Brunelle knew.

"Just like Mama Maggie said," Carlisle recalled.

Brunelle frowned at the screen. "But there's no information here. It's a kiss with no promise."

Carlisle wrinkled her nose at the metaphor. "What the hell does that mean?"

"It means we need more," Brunelle explained.

"A little sex-offender-y there, Dave," Carlisle observed. "You might want to come up with a less aggressive metaphor than a girl not giving you more than a kiss."

"Yeah, that's probably true," Brunelle admitted as he started to write the case numbers onto a piece of scrap paper. "Now, let's see if the clerk can pull the paper files on these."

The clerk in question, a middle-aged man with glasses, a beard, and a flannel shirt over a beer belly took the scrap of paper and offered an uninspiring, "I'll see what I can find," before disappearing into the back area behind the main counter.

"I hope this gives us something," Brunelle tapped on the counter anxiously. He felt like he needed a win to give him momentum going into the argument against dismissing an entire murder case because he shot off his mouth.

Carlisle agreed and leaned against the counter. She didn't seem anxious. But like she said, if Brunelle lost a motion based on his own misconduct, he'd lose that alone.

Eventually, the clerk emerged from the back. His hands were noticeably empty of files.

"Sorry," he said. "Those files are all sealed. I'm not able to provide them to the public."

"Well, we're not just the public," Brunelle tried. "We're county prosecutors."

"King County," Carlisle put in. Candid prosecutor.

"Uh, yes. King County," Brunelle admitted.

"That's okay," the clerk said. "I don't care if you're big shots from Seattle. I wouldn't give them to our local prosecutors either. They're unavailable to anyone, by order of the court."

Gears started to turn in Brunelle's mind. "Which judge?"

If a judge sealed the files, he could always unseal them. Even if it was at the request of a couple of carpet-bagging bigshots from Seattle.

But the clerk shook his head. "That's sealed too. I don't even know."

"You mean to tell me," Carlisle asked, "that you have court records that are supposed to be public, but have been sealed away from public view by a judge, but we can't ask the judge to undo it because there's no way to know which judge did it, because they sealed their name too?"

The clerk took a moment to make sure he understood each part of Carlisle's lengthy lawyer question. Then he nodded. "Yup."

"That's bullshit," Carlisle observed.

"There's no need to curse, ma'am," the clerk complained. "I'm just doing my job."

"Ignore the cursing," Brunelle offered. "It's part of her charm. Really. Thank you for your help." Polite prosecutor.

Brunelle led Carlisle outside and they took a moment to regroup on the courthouse steps.

"There can't be that many judges in this county," Brunelle surmised. "It's based on population, and this isn't exactly urban. We could probably narrow it down to a few likely candidates."

"Or just take it in front of any judge down here," Carlisle suggested. "The one who actually sealed those records is probably retired by now anyway."

"I hope not," Brunelle replied. "No judge is going to want to undo another judge's decision to seal records."

"Not without knowing why it was sealed," Carlisle agreed, "which is something we can't know."

"Because they're sealed," Brunelle finished their thought.

He sighed. He was hungry, despite the knot in his stomach that hadn't ever fully faded since Nicole read him the title of Ryder's motion. They needed to head north.

"Let's get out of here and think about the best way to follow up," he suggested. "We've got a few weeks still before the trial, but..." He trailed off.

"But you've only got six days to keep our case from getting dismissed," Carlisle said it out loud, "or none of this matters anyway."

"Our case?" Brunelle grinned. "I thought I was in this alone."

"Only if you lose." Carlisle smiled back at her partner. "If we win, we win together. So, let's win."

CHAPTER 13

Brunelle spent the better part of the next three days drafting his response to Ryder's motion to dismiss. He could have assigned part of it to Carlisle, or even made her do the entire thing, but she was right: it was his mess. He needed to be the one to clean it up.

He wasn't a fan of legal writing. That was part of what made criminal practice so appealing. There was a lot less paper and a lot more courtroom. He was able to muster up a passable response, but he didn't have the expertise that a civil lawyer like Ryder would have in burying an opponent, and thereby also the court, in densely written pleadings. Brunelle thought that might actually be an advantage. Judges were busy people. They didn't want to wade through pages upon pages of flowery arguments. They wanted to hurry up and make a decision so they could hurry up and get to the next decision they had to make, and the one after that, and so on. Brunelle kept his written response concise. Ryder's motion had been 20 pages long. Brunelle's response was six, and that included the signature page. Sometimes, less was more, and simpler was better. He just hoped this would be one of those times.

The court administrators scheduled the hearing in front of Judge Michael Martinez. It was a good draw for Brunelle. There were 52 judges on the King County Superior Court. That was 49 more than the three judges on the Grays Harbor County Superior Court, but then King County had a lot more cases to hear. In fact, King was such a big county that they divided the cases into categories—adult criminal, juvenile, civil, family, etc.—and then assigned judges to hear just those types of cases for rotations that could last anywhere from one to five years. The judges came from all different types of backgrounds, roughly corresponding to those same practice areas. That meant, say, a family law case could end up in front of a judge who had never handled a family law case in their entire pre-judge career. Fortunately, Martinez had been a criminal practitioner before ascending to the bench. Even more fortunately, he had been a prosecutor.

Not that Brunelle expected Judge Martinez to side with him just because they had been on the same team once. It was just that Martinez would understand the nuances of criminal plea bargaining. And, hopefully, how the law of contracts not only did not, but should not, apply to it.

"All rise!" the bailiff called out to begin the hearing. "The King County Superior Court is now in session, The Honorable Michael Martinez presiding."

Everyone was duly assembled for the hearing on Ryder's motion to dismiss. Brunelle and Carlisle sat at the prosecutors' table. Ryder and Strunk were at the defendant's table. Normally in a murder case, there would also be two jail guards who had transported the defendant from his cell and were guarding the exits should he make any moves to try not to return to it. But Ryder had convinced the last judge to set the bail so low that

Daddy Strunk had posted it. Strunk was walking free and sat at the defense table in a suit and tie looking like he was just another lawyer. Brunelle hoped Ryder wouldn't be quite so persuasive this next time.

"Are the parties ready," Judge Martinez asked after he sat down on the bench, "on the matter of the State of Washington versus Maximillian Strunk?"

Brunelle stood to answer first. The prosecutor always answered first. And lawyers always stood when addressing the judge. "The State is ready, Your Honor."

Ryder stood next. "The defense is ready as well, Your Honor."

"All right then, good," Martinez said. He took a moment to organize some papers on the bench, then looked up again. "I have read all of the briefing and generally familiarized myself with the procedural history of the case. This motion was brought by the defense and so the burden of persuasion is on them. Accordingly, I will hear first from Mr. Ryder. Whenever you're ready, counsel."

Ryder stood up again and stepped out from behind the defense table and into the well at the center of the courtroom. It was a strange move for oral argument on a legal motion. There was no jury to impress; theatrics were unnecessary. Brunelle found it off-putting. He hoped the judge shared his sentiment.

"This is a motion about justice, Your Honor," Ryder began. "Justice is supposed to be the guiding principle of the Prosecutor's Office, but it appears Mr. Brunelle does not personally share in that most laudable of goals."

Here we go. Brunelle rolled his eyes slightly. Again, no jurors present, so he didn't have to watch his facial expressions quite as much. Although reacting negatively to a personal attack would suggest disagreement with it, so he was probably safe if the judge noticed it.

"Thankfully," Ryder continued, "Mr. Strunk and his attorney know that this Court has no greater interest than preserving his rights to due process and equal justice before the law. It is for that reason that we are confident the Court will grant our motion to enforce the plea agreement entered into by Mr. Brunelle on behalf of the State, and dismiss the charges against Mr. Strunk."

"He left off the murder part," Carlisle whispered. "I feel like that's important."

Brunelle nodded. "In theory, it shouldn't matter what the charge is," he whispered back, "but in reality, yeah, I think it will."

"As the Court knows," Ryder continued, "my client has been charged with a most serious crime for doing nothing more than exercising his legal right to defend another citizen. The right to defense of others has a long history in our jurisprudence and is specifically codified in our law at Revised Code of Washington 9A.16.020. It is true that my client's actions that fateful night led to the death of William Harrison Welles, a giant of our legal community, but it is also true that his actions were not criminal. And I dare suggest, Mr. Welles himself would be the first to argue as much were he alive today."

But he's not, Brunelle thought, *because your client killed him.*

"This is not a case where a defendant comes up with some flimsy defense after being tracked down and backed into a factual corner," Ryder asserted. "No. In this case, Mr. Strunk voluntarily spoke with detectives. He admitted to the acts which led to Mr. Welles's death. And he explained why he had no choice but to do what he did. He explained, in his own words, that he acted in the defense of his friend. Mr. Strunk may not have known about Revised Code of Washington 9A.16.020, but Detective Chen should have. And Mr. Brunelle undoubtedly does."

"That last bit is true," Brunelle whispered to Carlisle. She grinned but didn't reply.

"Which is why, when he and I first discussed the case, our negotiations immediately turned to the issue of defense of others. Mr. Brunelle admitted that if what my client said was true—and of course it was—then he would not be guilty of any crime and the case should be dismissed. The only issue was one of corroboration. I don't fault Mr. Brunelle for wanting some confirmation of Mr. Strunk's claims, and so it was mutually agreed upon that he would hear from the only other witness to the event, my other client Jonathan Beckle."

Judge Martinez raised a surprised hand at Ryder. "Hold on. You represent both Mr. Strunk and Mr. Beckle?"

"Yes, Your Honor," Ryder admitted. "I proudly represent both men involved in this tragedy."

Martinez frowned down from the bench. "You don't think that might be a conflict of interest?"

Ryder shook his head. "Absolutely not, Your Honor, for neither man is guilty of any crime. Their interests are aligned. Both regret what happened that night, and both seek justice, just as does this Honorable Court."

The judge frowned deeper at the obvious flattery, but he relented. "All right then. You may continue."

"Thank you, Your Honor. As I was saying, Mr. Brunelle offered, and I agreed, that he should hear from Mr. Beckle, and if Mr. Beckle corroborated Mr. Strunk's version of events, then Mr. Brunelle would dismiss the charges against Mr. Strunk. This was not an extraordinary offer, nor would it be an outrageous result.

If all of the witnesses to an event provide a description that is not a crime under the law, then no charges should follow. And so, we agreed."

Ryder paused, apparently for dramatic effect because he then raised a professorial finger at the judge.

"Allow me to take a moment at this juncture in my presentation, to review a few of the basics of the law of contracts we all learned in our first year of law school."

Oh dear, Brunelle thought.

"A contract is an agreement between two parties," Ryder said, "a meeting of the minds, as we say, supported by the exchange of something of value, which we lawyers call the consideration. As soon as you have that meeting of the minds and that consideration, a contract exists, regardless of whether it is ever reduced to writing. That old saying about an oral contract being worth the paper it's written on is a comment on the evidentiary difficulty of proving such a contract, not on the actual existence of it. And so it was here that Mr. Strunk, through his attorney, and the State of Washington, through its attorney Mr. Brunelle, entered into a legal and binding contract. The meeting of the minds was the agreement that if and when Mr. Beckle corroborated Mr. Strunk's statement, then the State would dismiss the charges against Mr. Strunk. The consideration was the production of Mr. Beckle to make such a statement."

"Wouldn't the consideration be the statement itself, Mr. Ryder?" Judge Martinez interrupted. "That is, assuming I agree that contract law has any applicability to a criminal case."

Ryder raised that finger a bit higher. "Ah, yes, one might think it was the statement itself, Your Honor, but Mr. Brunelle's subsequent actions at the time that statement was proffered show that it was not the statement itself which mattered, but rather the willingness and present ability to present it. When we showed up for that interview, we had substantially complied with our portion of the contract. Mr. Brunelle could not then frustrate the consummation of the contract by refusing to allow us to provide the agreed upon consideration."

"I feel like I kind of could," Brunelle whispered to Carlisle.

"You should probably just pay attention at this point, Dave," she whispered back. "I can't tell if Martinez might be buying this horseshit."

"There is another doctrine in contract law," Ryder continued, "called anticipatory breach of contract. An anticipatory breach of contract occurs when one party—Mr. Brunelle—commits some action—refusing to ask Mr. Beckle about what happened that evening, as agreed—that shows the party's intention to fail to fulfill its contractual obligations to the other party—dismissal of the charges. We could not get to an actual full breach of the contract, because Mr. Brunelle breached the contract in advance. But whether an actual breach or an anticipatory breach, there is no conclusion other than that Mr. Brunelle breached the contract."

Brunelle thought there was probably another conclusion.

"When there is a breach of contract, as here," Ryder went on, "the remedy depends on the nature of the contract and the parties. In the commercial realm, the preferred remedy is monetary damages. The court determines what the breach cost the aggrieved party and orders the breaching party to pay that amount, in an effort to put the innocent party in the same position they would have been without the breach. That should be the same intent here, but money cannot substitute for the benefit Mr. Strunk was to receive for fulfilling his part of the bargain. What use is money to a man spending his life in prison for a crime he didn't commit?"

"Cigarettes?" Carlisle suggested under her breath.

Brunelle stifled a chuckle. He knew he was about to have to stand up and defend his actions.

"No," Ryder jabbed that finger into the air. "The only remedy for this breach of contract is specific performance of the terms of the contract. The Court must order the State to take the actions necessary to fulfill its obligations under the contract. Or rather, the Court can, should, and must step in and effectuate that result. The Court must give Mr. Strunk the benefit of his bargain. The Court must dismiss this case. Thank you."

Ryder turned on his heel and stepped sharply back to his seat. Brunelle was about to stand up to speak, but Martinez wasn't quite done with Ryder.

"How do I know, Mr. Ryder," he questioned, "that Mr. Beckle was going to actually corroborate Mr. Strunk's version of events?"

Ryder stood up again. "That is quite simple, Your Honor. I would not have produced him for the interview if he hadn't been going to do so."

Conflict of interest or not, Brunelle had to admit that rang true.

Martinez nodded at the response as well. "All right, then." He turned to the prosecution table. "Who will be delivering the argument on behalf of the State?"

There would have been grounds to have Carlisle argue the response to Ryder's motion. As the saying went, a person who represents himself has a fool for a client. But it might also have made Brunelle look unconfident in his actions. 'Consciousness of guilt' was the name of the doctrine prosecutors regularly argued to juries about what inferences to draw from a suspect running from the cops or fleeing a crime scene. He was sure as hell going to argue it at Strunk's trial when they all watched the surveillance video of Strunk and Beckle running out of Welles's office building, leaving him to bleed out on the floor rather than call 9-1-1 for help. Brunelle was willing to stand his ground and answer questions about his actions. He was just going to tell the judge it was none of his damn business.

"I will, Your Honor." Brunelle stood up, chin raised.

Martinez smiled slightly and nodded to him. "Whenever you're ready, Mr. Brunelle."

"Thank you, Your Honor," Brunelle said. Then he began. "While plea bargains have some analogies to contracts, contract law has no place in the realm of criminal law, nor, Your Honor, should it. As Mr. Ryder alluded to at the end of his argument, the usual remedy in a contract dispute is money, and not only does money have no utility to either side in a criminal case, the introduction of the very idea of it is so improper as to be repulsive. Contract law is about money. Criminal law is about justice."

Brunelle did not step out from behind his table. He didn't want to repeat Ryder's distracting move, and he really didn't; want Martinez to think he felt a need to copy his opponent. This was an intellectual argument, not an emotional one, and he wanted the judge to feel that as he considered his ruling.

"Your Honor," Brunelle continued, "I could engage Mr. Ryder's arguments about contract law. I could argue whether I have the authority to enter into an enforceable contract on behalf of the entire State of Washington. I could argue whether there was truly a meeting of the minds as to what the bargain was or should have been. I could argue whether the consideration in this case was the agreement to produce Mr. Beckle for a statement, or his provision of such statement, or the content of such a statement. I could argue whether Mr. Ryder refusing to allow his client—I'm sorry, his other client, Mr. Beckle—to answer any questions other than what he expected constituted an anticipatory breach on his part, rather than mine. And I could argue whether dismissal of a murder charge is truly the appropriate remedy for any alleged breach of an alleged contract, or whether some lesser remedy might suffice. But I am not going to argue any of that."

"It kind of sounds like you just did, Mr. Brunelle," Judge Martinez interjected.

Brunelle smiled slightly. Of course he did. He couldn't completely ignore his opponent's arguments. He just preferred to make them irrelevant.

"Perhaps I did, Your Honor," Brunelle allowed, "but I need not have. The law is clear, Your Honor. The criminal case law. The prosecution may revoke a plea bargain offer at any time up to the formal acceptance of that bargain by the Court. Like it or not, fair or not, I can pull a plea offer just because I want to, just because I changed my mind. Even if I offer it at the pretrial conference, and the defendant accepts it, and we schedule it for a plea hearing, and everyone shows up and the guilty plea form is all filled out and signed by the defendant and his lawyer, I can still say, 'Nah, never mind.' Is that fair? I don't know. Maybe, maybe not. But is it the law? Absolutely."

Brunelle stole a glance over at Ryder. He couldn't help but want to know how his opponent was reacting to his argument. Ryder was staring right at him, his frustration barely concealed. Perfect.

"I do stand prepared to answer any questions the Court

might have about what happened when Mr. Ryder brought his one client to provide a statement in support of his other client," Brunelle offered. "And I am prepared to answer questions about why we would want to know some background about his relationship with the dead man—like, why were they even there that night?—before weighing the credibility of any claims about the events in question. But again, I don't believe I need to. I would urge this criminal court, sitting over a criminal case, ruling on a motion under the criminal rules, to apply the criminal case law, and deny the defendant's motion to dismiss. Thank you."

Brunelle sat down quickly, lest Martinez actually ask him any of those questions. Doing so would signal some openness to follow Ryder's arguments rather than Brunelle's. He waited anxiously to see whom the judge addressed next.

He turned to Ryder. "Any reply, counsel?"

Brunelle exhaled a sigh of relief. But quietly. He wasn't looking to attract the judge's attention back to him.

Ryder stood up and took a moment to gather his thoughts. "Well, Your Honor, I suppose my reply is that it is not surprising Mr. Brunelle doesn't want to talk about the merits of my contentions. He knows he made an agreement. He knows he intentionally frustrated that agreement. And he knows if he had allowed the interview to go forward, then he would have been compelled to dismiss the case. That's nothing more than buyer's remorse, Your Honor. But buyer's remorse doesn't get you out of the contract. That's why the buyer is remorseful. He's stuck with the bargain he struck. And so is Mr. Brunelle. We urge you to dismiss this case."

He sat down again, and everyone sat forward, awaiting the ruling from on high.

Judge Martinez stood up. "I will take a few minutes to

deliberate on my decision," he announced. "Court will be at recess for fifteen minutes."

"All rise!" the bailiff called out, and everyone stood as the judge disappeared into his chambers.

"Is this good?" Carlisle wondered aloud.

Brunelle shrugged. "Mysterious ways."

"I think that's God who works in mysterious ways," Carlisle commented.

"In this courtroom," Brunelle answered, "the judge is God."

There was an opportunity to engage with Ryder. 'Good argument' and a handshake or something. Brunelle would have done that with Edwards, perhaps, although she likely wouldn't have appreciated a show of familiarity like that in front of her client. Such potential discomfort between Ryder and Strunk was the only reason Brunelle even considered it, but he decided to just keep his back to his opponent and wait out the next excruciating fourteen minutes talking to Carlisle. They did have things to discuss.

"What are we going to do about those records in Grays Harbor?" he asked, keeping his voice low lest Ryder overhear.

"We should schedule a motion to unseal, I guess," Carlisle suggested. "The tricky part will be how. We don't know who the judge was and we don't work at the Prosecutor's Office that represented the State at that previous hearing."

"We should probably ask the Grays Harbor County Prosecutor's Office to file the motion to unseal," Brunelle considered. "We would want them to do that courtesy to us if the roles were reversed."

Carlisle nodded. "Agreed. I can reach out to them, if you want."

Brunelle considered. He wasn't the best at delegating tasks. Part of the reason was that he felt bad giving what he considered his work to other people. Another part of it was an underlying belief that no one else could do his work as well as him. But he knew better when it came to Carlisle. She did his work better than him, and she wanted to be part of the effort. That was why he'd asked her to be his co-counsel again.

"Okay, thanks," he agreed. "Let me know what they say."

Carlisle offered a "Will do," and then they waited for Martinez to reemerge. When he did, the bailiff let out with another "All rise!" A few moments later, they were ready for the ruling. Maybe they wouldn't have to bother reaching out to the Grays Harbor County Prosecutor's Office after all.

"Please be seated," Judge Martinez instructed as he did the same. "I'd like to start by thanking both counsel for their well-considered arguments and professional presentations. This is an interesting issue, and one I have not seen presented quite like this before."

Brunelle hoped that was a good thing.

"I think the reason why I've never quite seen this before," Martinez continued, "is for the reasons Mr. Brunelle argued. It has been generally accepted that a prosecutor can withdraw an offer at any time, and therefore it has probably been generally accepted by the defense bar that they have little to no recourse when an offer is pulled."

Yes, a good thing, he thought, but only for a moment.

"However," Martinez cautioned, "it sometimes takes an outsider to bring a fresh perspective. Mr. Ryder's expertise falls perhaps more on the civil side of the law, but it is this experience which allows him to see this disagreement in a different way, and I do not think it inappropriate or frivolous to ask the Court to try to see it in that way as well. Just because the rule has always been that prosecutors can act with impunity doesn't mean this Court should condone such impunity."

Impunity was a bad thing, Brunelle knew. The kind of thing a judge might want to take down. He braced himself for the remainder of the judge's ruling.

"Therefore," Martinez announced, "I am going to base my ruling wholly apart from Mr. Brunelle's argument that he could withdraw his offer at any time."

Uh-oh. Definitely bad.

"Instead, I am going to accept Mr. Ryder's invitation to analyze this controversy through the lens of contract law," the judge said.

"Thank you, Your Honor," Ryder stood up and interjected.

Martinez smiled slightly. "Don't thank me yet."

Or maybe good.

Ryder sat down again, a bit deflated.

"In order for a party to be entitled to a remedy under contract law," Judge Martinez explained, "four criteria must be met. First, a contract must actually exist. Second, the aggrieved party must have performed according to the terms of the contract. Third, the other party must have breached the contract by not fulfilling its obligations. And fourth, the aggrieved party must have suffered some damage as a result of that breach. So, I will analyze each of these in turn, although not necessarily in order."

Brunelle took a deep breath. He often wondered why judges didn't deliver their rulings at the beginning of their remarks, and then explain their reasoning afterward. But he knew it was because both lawyers would stop listening immediately, and one of them would start arguing.

"So, first of all, was there a contract in this case?" Martinez posed the question to himself. "I think there was. Regardless of the exact words stated, there seems to have been an understanding that a statement by Mr. Beckle that corroborated the version of events as told by Mr. Strunk would render further prosecution of the case either unwarranted or impractical.

"Jumping to the last criteria," Martinez continued, "was Mr. Strunk damaged by the failure of the contract to be carried out? Well, I think that is true as well. The case has not been dismissed. He sits here today, proof that he did not receive the benefit of the bargain he had hoped for."

Brunelle supposed both of those things were true.

"So, the real question lies in who breached the contract," Martinez said. "Did Mr. Brunelle breach it by refusing to ask about the incident, which was after all supposed to be the subject of the statement? Or did Mr. Ryder breach it by terminating the interview before those questions could be asked? That I think is the crux of this case, and it is the resolution of that issue which will determine my decision."

Brunelle nodded slightly, not because he necessarily agreed, but because he wanted the judge to continue.

But he didn't. He just sat on the bench, fingers steepled in thought. Making everyone wait. Which everyone did. No one dared interrupt him, lest such disrespect tip the scales against them.

Brunelle's heart started to beat heavier in his chest. He glanced at Carlisle, but all she could offer was a slight shrug as she too waited for Martinez to say something. Anything.

Finally, he spoke. "And the truth is, I'm not sure. I don't know. It seems to me that both of you likely failed to do what you promised. I am not persuaded either way. Which means, since the defendant brought this motion and in doing so bore the burden of persuasion, I will find that he has failed to meet that burden. The motion to dismiss is denied."

Brunelle had never felt better about being so close to losing. The burden of proof was usually a sword wielded against him at trial. It was nice to hide behind it like a shield for once.

"I will prepare written findings," Martinez announced before there could be any argument from the defense table. "Will the parties be prepared to begin the trial as scheduled in two weeks' time?"

"Yes, Your Honor," Brunelle hurried to answer, to encourage the conversation to move on from any challenge to the ruling he had just won.

Ryder stood up. He had two choices. Argue and complain, or stand tall and accept the challenge. "The defense will be ready, Your Honor."

Martinez accepted the responses from the lawyers and stepped off the bench. Brunelle started to gather his things, but Ryder came over to interrupt him.

"You dodged a bullet there, Brunelle."

Brunelle turned to face his opponent. "I wish I could say the same for Mr. Welles."

Ryder sneered. "Oh, very cute. Are you going to say something unethical like that in your opening statement too?"

"Unethical?" Brunelle thought his remark was clever, and darkly funny, but hardly unethical.

"You don't fool me, Brunelle." Ryder apparently decided to show just how much of a sore loser he was. "You reneged on our deal. You can tell the judge or the jury whatever you want, but that was a breach of your ethical duties to another lawyer. I'll wait until the trial is over, but once that jury says, 'Not Guilty',

I'm going to have your bar card."

Brunelle knew civil attorneys were far more accustomed to personal attacks on opposing counsel. That didn't mean he was just going to take it.

"You're going to file a bar complaint against me," he asked, "for beating you in a motion hearing?"

"You're damn right I am," Ryder threatened. "Unless you want to honor your end of the bargain after all. Mr. Beckle is still willing to tell you that Mr. Strunk did nothing wrong."

"I'm sure he is," Brunelle laughed. "But how are you going to convince the Bar I did something wrong if you couldn't convince the judge just now?"

"Ha! The judge wasn't going to dismiss a murder case," Ryder scoffed. "That's the only reason you won. You heard him. It was a close call. He wanted to rule in my favor. He just didn't want to be responsible for dumping a first-degree murder charge."

Brunelle crossed his arms and appraised his opponent. Strunk and Carlisle were both watching intently, as was the bailiff, but none of them deigned to jump in.

"Are you also going to seek sanctions against me?" Brunelle suggested. "Isn't that what you civil guys do? Insult each other on the record and in pleadings? Ask for sanctions? File bar complaints?"

Ryder's eyes narrowed a bit. "I didn't know you could ask for sanctions on a criminal case."

"You can't!" Brunelle barked. "This isn't about money. And it isn't about you and it isn't about me. It's about justice. It's about murder and holding a killer responsible. It's about justice."

"Justice means honoring your contracts," Ryder tried.

Brunelle laughed. "Fuck you and fuck your contracts.

Fuck your sanctions and your bar complaints.. He jabbed a finger toward Ryder's chest. "You're the one who's representing both the murderer and the key witness. You're the one with the huge conflict of interest you can't see. You think that won't blow up in your face at some point? It will, and when it does, it won't be me filing a bar complaint against you, it'll be that guy," he pointed over Ryder's shoulder at Strunk, "or his buddy. Maybe both. Because when push comes to shove and this trial starts, each of them is going to decide to save their own sorry butt, and that potential conflict of interest you think they've waived is going to explode into a very real, very unwaivable conflict of interest. If anyone is going to lose their bar card at the end of this, it's not me, Ryder. It's not me."

"Bravo!" Carlisle called out from behind Brunelle, clapping her hands. "Now get out of here before we file a motion or something on your ass."

Ryder just shook his head at them. "Unethical and overconfident. Perfect. I will enjoy beating you at trial."

Brunelle searched for yet another snappy comeback, but failed to do so before Ryder turned and grabbed his client by the arm. "Come on, Max. Let's leave these two to their misery."

Brunelle watched them head for the exit, then turned to Carlisle. "I don't feel miserable. Are you miserable?"

"I am not miserable," Carlisle confirmed. "But that guy is a miserable piece of shit."

Brunelle could hardly disagree. Even Welles, in all his vainglory and bombast, had never threatened to file a bar complaint because he lost a motion. Ryder's tantrum just made Brunelle want to win the case that much more. Which was why they really needed to figure out why Beckle and Strunk had gone to Welles's office that night. He was sure it wasn't just an innocent consultation gone wrong. And he was sure it had something to do with those sealed files in Grays Harbor County.

Beckle might not have talked to Chen, or to Brunelle, but he was going to talk to the jury. Conflict of interest or no, Ryder was going to put him on the stand to say Strunk was just defending him. Brunelle needed ammunition to attack Beckle. He needed those files unsealed.

The trial was scheduled to begin in two weeks. He smiled at his co-counsel. He was sure Carlisle would manage to get the contents of those files before the end of those two weeks.

He was wrong.

CHAPTER 14

"Four weeks?" Brunelle practically shouted. "They set the hearing in four weeks?"

"That's what they told me," Carlisle answered.

They were in Brunelle's office. Carlisle had come up to break the bad news.

"Did they say why?" Brunelle demanded.

"I asked," Carlisle shrugged, "but they didn't really have an answer for me. 'It's just how we do things down here,' they said."

"Did you ask them to do it faster?" Brunelle asked. "Prosecutor to prosecutor?"

"I did," Carlisle confirmed.

"And?"

"Four weeks."

"Fuck." Brunelle hissed.

"Agreed," Carlisle responded. "Although, on the other hand, we don't actually know any of those cases had anything to do with Beckle."

"It would be nice to know that now," Brunelle said,

"before we have to give opening statement."

"Well, the good news is, we probably won't be done with our trial before they argue their motion," Carlisle pointed out.

Brunelle considered. "Yeah, probably not. But who knows if we'll actually get a ruling then, or if it'll be another four weeks before the judge decides to unseal those records."

"Or the judge might decide not to unseal them at all," Carlisle pointed out. "We can't rely on anything that we think might be in there. We might be wrong."

Brunelle nodded, considering his options. "Well, let's hope we're right. And let's hope we get proof of that before Jonathan Beckle takes the stand."

* * *

The two weeks before the trial flew by, as they were wont to do. There was a lot to do and not enough time to do it. At least that's how it always felt. But it always came to the same situation. Trial to begin on Monday morning, and Brunelle sipping a glass of bourbon before an early bedtime on Sunday night.

He had prepared all he could prepare and tomorrow the battle would be joined. He knew that Strunk was defending Beckle, or at the very least, Beckle had created the need to be defended. The law might let you defend yourself or others, but not if you were the first aggressor. You couldn't pick a fight and then kill someone because you were losing. That would be Brunelle's argument. He didn't have another one.

He took a sip of bourbon and stared out at the city lights of the Emerald City. He knew even then, hidden beneath the beauty of the twinkling lights reflecting off the water, there were people being robbed, assaulted, even killed. It wasn't his night to be on call—not the night before trial—but when it was time again, there would be a body. Another poor soul lying face up and dead-eyed in a pool of his own blood. Another Welles.

Brunelle wondered what was in those files down in the courthouse in Montesano. Welles had always been one of the worst defense attorneys to deal with. He could hardly imagine Welles doing anything good for anyone else. But Lady Blackwell had said he was not just a donor, but a financial lifeline. Apparently there was more than met the eye to William Harrison Welles. Billy.

Brunelle decided the jury needed to meet Billy. They might not care about a blowhard like William Harrison Welles dying at the hand of one of his own clients. But little Billy Welles, the orphan who grew up to give back, that kid was a hero. And only villains killed heroes.

Brunelle took another sip and looked out one more time at the hidden deluge of criminality he knew was cowering just out of sight. He couldn't actually do anything to stop it. He owed his living to people hurting other people. But one case at a time, he could try to bring some small semblance of justice to the world.

Even on behalf of William Harrison Welles.

Especially on behalf of William Harrison Welles.

CHAPTER 15

The first day of trial was like the first day at a new school or a new job. Not much of substance actually happened. It was all about getting oriented, and getting ready to do the real work the next day. The most important thing to happen was for the case to be assigned out to a particular judge for trial. Which of those 52 judges would preside over the trial of Maximillian Strunk? Jacoby and Martinez had already handled small parts of it. Would they get the trial or would it be, like it usually was, a completely different judge? Brunelle and Ryder appeared at the Criminal Presiding Courtroom at 8:30 a.m. that Monday morning to find out who their judge would be. At least one of them would be disappointed, with an outside chance they both were. The only thing worse than a judge with a prejudice for one side or another on a criminal case was a judge who had so little experience in criminal matters to have such an opinion.

And that was exactly who they got.

Judge Anders Holmsund. By all accounts a perfectly nice fellow, but with absolutely no experience in criminal cases. Even less than Ryder. He'd been a partner at the firm of Holmsund &

Lundgren, a municipal land use firm founded by his grandfather and another of Seattle's wave of Swedish immigrants. At least he had run for and been elected judge, rather than having been appointed because his firm donated enough to the governor's reelection campaign. But he had won mostly on name recognition—or name origin recognition—and not due to any particular ability or talent to be a judge.

The question was whether Holmsund was open to being educated by the attorneys, or would see such openness as a weakness to hide from the litigants before him. That was, would he listen to Brunelle, who knew criminal law better than anyone else in the courtroom, or would he buck against Brunelle's obviously superior knowledge and experience in order to establish his unearned dominance over the courtroom?

Time would tell. Brunelle wasn't optimistic.

"Who did we get?" Carlisle asked as she walked into the courtroom a minute after the selection was made.

"Holmsund," Brunelle answered.

"Fuck," Carlisle opined.

Brunelle was inclined to agree. "Come on," he said. "Holmsund's courtroom is on the eighth floor. Let's see how bad it is."

* * *

In the event, it wasn't that bad at all. Holmsund definitely had no business presiding over a murder trial, but he seemed to understand that himself. He was going to rely on the attorneys after all. And that meant he was going to rely even more on Brunelle and Carlisle.

"Good morning, everyone!" Judge Holmsund practically sang as he took the bench after his clerk's obligatory call of, "All rise!" He was young for a judge, probably about 40, with brown hair that hadn't started graying yet, a clean-shaven baby face, and a slight frame barely holding up the black wool robe of the judge he had somehow managed to become. "Is everyone ready to get started?"

It was a little less formal than the, 'Are the parties ready on the matter of *The State of Washington versus Maximillian Andrew Strunk*?' which Brunelle had come to expect. But he decided he could get used to it. Especially because he felt a growing confidence that he would be able to push Holmsund around even more than Ryder was certainly already planning to.

"The State is ready, Your Honor," Brunelle responded. "David Brunelle and Gwen Carlisle appearing on behalf of the State of Washington."

"The defense is ready as well, Your Honor," Ryder added. "Nathaniel Ryder on behalf of the accused, Maximillian Strunk."

"Thank you, counsels," Holmsund responded, but before he could say anything further, Ryder continued talking.

"In fact, Your Honor," he said," the defense would like to begin by asking this Honorable Court to reconsider an earlier motion regarding the defendant's motion for specific performance of a plea agreement. There are some additional arguments which, when considered by this Court, should change the outcome of that hearing."

And then Holmsund surprised everyone.

"You will not dictate the proceedings, Mr. Ryder," Holmsund warned him. He looked to the prosecution table. "Nor will the State. I am the judge and this is my courtroom. I will establish the order and duration of the proceedings. And the very first thing I will not do, Mr. Ryder, is overturn a ruling made by a previous judge after a full and fair hearing. We are not here for you to seek a second bite of the apple. We are here to conduct a trial in a fair and expeditious manner, and I am determined to make that, and nothing but that, occur."

All of the lawyers stood silent, stunned by the unexpected seizure of control of the courtroom.

"Am I understood?" Holmsund demanded.

Brunelle not only understood it, he welcomed it. His side was the one to benefit from a no-nonsense presentation of the facts and law, absent the manipulations of a civil litigator out of his element. "Absolutely, Your Honor," Brunelle answered for himself and Carlisle.

Ryder shifted his weight, then offered a curt nod. "Yes, Your Honor. Of course, Your Honor."

Holmsund smiled, but the boyish grin came across quite differently than when he had first taken the bench. He then proceeded to lay out the course of the trial. They would not be reconsidering any prior motions or rulings. They would address motions *in limine* that first day. Then they would bring in a panel of 80 prospective jurors. They would excuse anyone who would have a sufficient personal hardship that they could not sit for a multi-week criminal trial. From those who remained, they would seat twelve jurors and two alternates. Once the jury was selected, they would adjourn for the day, regardless of time, to allow both sides additional time to fine tune their opening statements. The trial would begin in earnest the next morning with the reading of preliminary instructions from the judge, followed by the opening statement of the prosecution.

Brunelle had no objections to that proposed course of action, and it wouldn't have mattered if he had. Holmsund kept everything on track. Accordingly, after a week of jury selection, with fourteen in the box and everyone assembled in what was very clearly his courtroom, Judge Holmsund completed his recitation of the preliminary instructions on the law, then announced, "Ladies and gentlemen of the jury, please give your attention to Mr. Brunelle who will deliver the opening statement on behalf of the State of Washington."

CHAPTER 16

Brunelle stood up and stepped out from behind the prosecution table. Carlisle could have given the opening statement, and there was some brief discussion of it when they were divvying up tasks for the trial. But opening statement was about painting a picture of what had happened, and Brunelle was the one who had seen it firsthand. Carlisle would give the closing argument. That was her strength anyway. Taking whatever mistakes the other side had made and stabbing them in the throat with them. In the interests of justice, of course.

Brunelle took up his usual spot in front of the jurors. There was a natural distance that people stood apart from each other when conversing. Although it might vary a bit from culture to culture, the important thing was to be aware of where it was and set up camp exactly there. Too close would feel aggressive and put the jurors on their heels. Too far would feel unconfident, which was the worst thing a lawyer could seem during opening statement. But that sweet spot—not too close and not too far— that signaled comfort. And in that setting, comfort would be presumed to flow from righteousness.

"You don't bring a gun to a fist fight," Brunelle began. "And you sure as heck don't bring a gun to an initial consultation with the best criminal defense attorney in Seattle."

He turned and gestured at Strunk. "But that's exactly what the defendant, Maximillian Strunk, did. He brought a gun to the office of William Harrison Welles, attorney at law. And a few short minutes later, Welles lay on his office floor, bleeding to death from four gunshots to the torso. And Mr. Strunk fled into the night, identified only because of the surveillance cameras in the lobby of the office building."

There was more to the story, to be sure. He hadn't even mentioned Beckle yet. But he wanted to control the narrative right at the beginning.

"Mr. Welles was the one minding his own business that night, quite literally. He was in his office—a second home to a successful workaholic attorney. And it was Mr. Strunk who brought a gun there. Mr. Strunk brought a gun into Mr. Welles's second home. And then he murdered him there."

Brunelle knew Ryder would get a chance to address the jury before the first witness took the stand, and he knew what Ryder was going to say. He was going to paint a different picture. One of a frightened young man only trying to protect his friend. But Brunelle wanted to be the one to frame that painting, so that no matter what Ryder threw at the canvas, the jury wouldn't be able to forget that Strunk had come to Welles's place, and had done so armed.

"Allow me to back up a bit," Brunelle continued, "and provide a larger context of what happened that evening. There were actually three people involved in the incident that evening, and it was late in the evening. Almost midnight, in fact. The first of these was Mr. Welles. As I mentioned, he was a successful attorney here in town. In fact, his office—the office where this murder took place—is only a few blocks down the hill from this very courthouse. That only makes sense, since he spent almost every day inside these walls, battling some prosecutor like me, representing his client to the best of his ability. And boy, did he have some ability."

Brunelle smiled and shook his head amiably. He wanted the jury to think he liked and respected Welles. He didn't. Not particularly. But a sympathetic victim was always better. He took a moment to gauge the reactions of the jurors. There were several smiles returned to him. *Good.*

"The next person I've mentioned is the defendant, Mr. Strunk," Brunelle continued. "He was there that night too. Obviously. He was the one who, by his own admission, put four slugs in Mr. Welles's chest. But let's come back to him, because there was a third person there that night. The person who was the bridge between the other two. That person is a man named Jonathan Beckle."

Brunelle would have preferred it if Beckle had been sitting next to Strunk, facing the same charges. Brunelle didn't have quite enough to charge him. But the trial had just begun. There was still time.

"Mr. Beckle was the one who wanted to speak with Mr. Welles," Brunelle explained. "Mr. Beckle was the one who had sought out Seattle's premier criminal defense attorney and insisted on meeting with him at nearly midnight. It was Mr. Beckle who needed a defense attorney for some reason. And it was Mr. Beckle who brought a friend with him. A friend armed with a semi-automatic pistol, concealed in his waistband. It was Mr. Beckle who knew things might go sideways and he was the one who told Mr. Strunk to bring that gun. And to be ready to use it."

Brunelle was stretching a bit on that last part. Opening statement was supposed to be a recitation of what the lawyer thought the evidence would show. That could include inferences, but it wasn't supposed to include guesses. Still, he had reason to believe he was probably correct about all that. And he doubted Ryder would be objecting to Brunelle making someone other than Strunk seem like the criminal mastermind behind the murder, whether he represented them both or not. Only Strunk was on trial. But again, there was still time.

"Mr. Strunk's only purpose in being there was to support Mr. Beckle, with deadly force as it turned out. So, what was Mr. Beckle's purpose in being there, you might ask. That, ladies and gentlemen, is a very good question. You would be forgiven if you expected to hear that Mr. Beckle had been charged with a crime and needed representation. After all, that's what Mr. Welles did, and he did it better than anybody."

Brunelle was having to swallow the bile at constantly complimenting someone he had actually rather disliked both professionally and personally in the time they had known each other. Welles certainly thought he was the best there was. Brunelle wasn't as convinced, but he was willing to give a dead man the benefit of the doubt. Since it suited his case.

"But you would also be mistaken," Brunelle went on. "One of the first things the investigators did in this case, after they identified the two men who ran from Mr. Welles's office as he lay dying on the floor, was to look up both men and see whether they had any pending or impending criminal cases. But neither of them did. There was, professionally speaking, no reason for either of them to meet with Mr. Welles. And there was even less reason to insist on doing it so late at night. It wasn't like Mr.

Beckle had an arraignment the next morning on some new criminal charge. No, the only reason to do it so late was to make sure there was no one else around."

Nefarious. Brunelle was pushing out past guessing and dipping his toe into innuendo. He knew if he went much further, Ryder would make him pay for it. He'd made his point anyway. He could pull back into the facts he did know for certain.

"As you might expect, things didn't go well. I won't say they didn't go as planned. Because Mr. Beckle planned to bring Mr. Strunk. And Mr. Strunk planned to bring a gun. Mr. Beckle spoke with Mr. Welles while Mr. Strunk took up a strategic position toward the back of the room. Eventually an argument broke out between Mr. Beckle and Mr. Welles, and Mr. Strunk decided to pull out the loaded gun he had brought into another man's second home, and he opened fire, killing Mr. Welles where he stood."

Brunelle took a moment to let that sink in. He wanted that image securely in the minds of the jurors as he finally addressed some of the weakness in his case.

"Now, one thing that's important to remember as you listen to the testimony in this case," Brunelle cautioned, "is that Mr. Welles isn't here to tell his side of the story. We are necessarily restricted to what Mr. Strunk told investigators. And in that statement, Mr. Strunk admitted to everything I just told you. He came with Mr. Beckle. He brought a loaded gun. He shot and killed William Harrison Welles. Importantly, all of that is corroborated by other evidence in the case. Things like the surveillance video, the ballistics testing of his firearm, the autopsy. But there are a few things he claimed that aren't supported by the physical evidence. In fact, they are refuted by that evidence. And as you might expect, those are the things that go to the heart of his claim that he was only protecting his friend."

Brunelle took a step to one side. It signified he was moving to the next stage of his argument. It also allowed the jury a better view of Strunk as he prepared to call him a liar. He wanted the jurors to see Strunk squirm a little.

"First of all, Mr. Strunk knew he wasn't going to get away with shooting an unarmed man," Brunelle said, "so he concocted a story about Mr. Welles arming himself with his own handgun first. But since that wasn't true, Mr. Strunk couldn't quite get the details to line up with reality. He claimed Mr. Welles extracted the gun from his desk drawer, but said he did so after coming around in front of his desk. You'll see photographs of that desk. It was enormous. There is no way he could have reached back and extracted anything from any drawer, let alone a handgun.

"Then, Mr. Strunk realized his claim of defending his friend would be bolstered if he claimed Mr. Welles shot first. But that was a mistake, because firing a handgun leaves evidence. In fact, Mr. Strunk actually changed his story about this alleged gun in the middle of his statement when the detective reminded him that if Mr. Welles fired a semi-automatic, then a shell casing would have been ejected, and a ballistics expert would be able to distinguish that casing from the ones fired from Mr. Strunk's weapon. You will hear a recording of that interview and you will hear Mr. Strunk change his story when confronted with that. Suddenly, Mr. Welles's semi-auto became a revolver, which as you may know, does not eject its casings. How convenient."

A disdainful shake of his head, but not a sneer. Not yet.

"Also convenient was Mr. Strunk's story that when they fled the scene, they removed and disposed of Mr. Welles's alleged handgun, while keeping ahold of the actual murder weapon. So convenient as to be unbelievable. But the final inconsistency is the fact that neither Mr. Beckle nor Mr. Strunk were shot, but there was also no revolver bullet found lodged into a wall or anywhere else where this phantom bullet would have come to rest. There were four bullets recovered that night, ladies and gentlemen. One from Mr. Welles's body at autopsy, and three from the wall behind him, with his DNA on them from tearing through his body and exiting out of his back. And all four of them were fired from the gun recovered from Mr. Strunk after his arrest."

Brunelle took that step back and centered himself in front of the jurors again.

"So, what can we conclude from all of that?" he asked them. "Three things. First, Mr. Strunk shot and killed William Harrison Welles. Second, Mr. Strunk knew he had no legal justification to do so. And so, third, he lied about what drove him to pull that trigger. He wasn't defending anyone. He was there as a show of force and he showed that force, then lied about it. He murdered William Harrison Welles. And at the end of this trial, we will stand up again and ask you to return a verdict of guilty to the charge of murder in the first degree. Thank you."

Brunelle turned and made his way back to the prosecution table. Not a march, but confident stride. Those jurors watched everything.

"Good job," Carlisle whispered as he sat down. "Considering what you had to work with."

Brunelle nodded. It was always hard to tell a jury what happened when the only witness was also the defendant and you wanted the jurors to believe part of it, but not all of it. 'He's a liar, sort of.'

But there wasn't time to dwell on the weaknesses of his own opening statement. He needed to pay attention to whatever strengths might be in Ryder's.

"Now, ladies and gentlemen of the jury," Judge Holmsund instructed, "please give your attention to Mr. Ryder who will deliver the opening statement on behalf of the defendant."

CHAPTER 17

Ryder stood up and straightened his again very expensive-looking suit. He came out confidently from behind the defense table and gestured widely at Brunelle and Carlisle as he took up a similar spot before the jury.

"That was very entertaining," he began, "but then again, most fiction is."

He lowered his hand again and squared his shoulders to the jury box.

"This is a very simple case, with a very simple explanation," Ryder told the jury. "Mr. Strunk did shoot and kill William Welles that night. And it was also perfectly legal for him to do. It was a tragedy, but it wasn't a crime. It was not murder. And no amount of spin from a couple of career prosecutors will be able to change that."

Brunelle had wondered how long it would take Ryder to cast a personal attack. Not long at all.

"Mr. Strunk is a victim too. He was a victim of circumstance. Everything he did that night, he did to be a good friend, until he was faced with a situation none of us would ever want to be in, and had to make a choice none of us would ever want to be in, and had to make a choice none of us would ever want to make. It was literally a life-or-death decision, and he had less than a moment to make it. And while he regrets that someone lost his life, he would make the same decision again, because it was the right thing to do. It was the lawful defense of another person, which means it was not murder."

Ryder's opening statement was already more argument than statement. Brunelle could have objected as 'argumentative' and Holmsund probably would have sustained it, but it would have served little purpose. Jurors didn't understand the difference between statement and argument—a lot of lawyers struggled with it—and would think he was just being obstructionist, or worse, that he was bothered by Ryder's argument. It was better to let him have his say, then prove him wrong. If he could, that is.

"Let's start at the beginning, shall we?" Ryder invited. He began a slow pace to his left. There was something conversational about walking and talking, but it could also be distracting. Brunelle avoided it. Ryder seemed to be pulling it off, though. "A lot of what Mr. Brunelle just told you is actually accurate. Mr. Strunk did accompany his friend, Jonathan Beckle, to an appointment to meet an attorney named William Welles. Max didn't know what the appointment was about, and Jonathan didn't tell him. It was a private matter, as you can imagine. They were meeting with a well-respected lawyer who did indeed handle criminal cases. Max didn't know that, of course. He just knew his friend asked him to come along and he said yes, because that's what friends do."

Ryder had reached the end of the jury box and opened his stance back toward his client. Brunelle begrudgingly admired the timing and use of the physical space.

"Did Max bring a gun that night?" Ryder asked. "Yes. Yes, he did. Because this is America, and because Mr. Welles's office was in a rather shady neighborhood not too far from some of the ever-increasing homeless encampments the city is allowing to multiply throughout our downtown. That's a conversation for another time, but Max didn't feel safe going there, and he still has a constitutional right to carry a firearm. There was nothing illegal about him doing so. If there were," he gestured to the prosecution table, "you can be sure Mr. Brunelle would have told you as much in his opening statement. But he didn't. He just intimated there was something inherently criminal in my client exercising his rights. Just like the rest of his case is based on intimation and innuendo."

Not all of it, Brunelle thought.

"So, let's recast how this evening started, shall we? Jonathan needed to talk with a lawyer. The lawyer's office was in a bad part of town. Jonathan asked Max to come with him, so he did. And because it was in a bad part of town, he brought his perfectly legal firearm. That's how the evening began, and there's nothing wrong with any of that."

Brunelle glanced at the jury to see if they were buying it. It was hard to tell. There were some crossed arms, but also some receptive expressions. It was early. They hadn't made up their minds yet, which was good. They weren't supposed to. But Brunelle would have preferred a few more sets of crossed arms. Maybe even a frown or two. Ryder continued.

"It was a late appointment because that was when Mr. Welles suggested. He was a successful attorney with a court-driven practice. He couldn't meet clients during the day because he was in court. So, he suggested the late appointment, and Jonathan agreed. Just another reason to feel uneasy about the neighborhood. In fact, the building was locked for security reasons, and Mr. Welles had to come down to let them in. You'll see the surveillance video. You'll see that everyone was smiling and shaking hands and there was nothing sinister going on. And if Jonathan and Max were really planning something criminal, do you really think they would have just let their faces be seen on that video?"

Yes, Brunelle thought, *if they didn't know there were cameras.*

"So, they all went upstairs, and Jonathan began his consultation with Mr. Welles. Maximillian wasn't there for that, and he didn't want to eavesdrop, so he sat down in a chair on the opposite side of the office. It was a big office. He started looking at his phone and ignored what was going on between Jonathan and Mr. Welles. As far as he knew, everything was fine. He was probably thinking about where they could stop for some food on the way home. And then…"

Ryder stopped the pacing again. He'd timed it to be exactly in the center of the jury box again. Brunelle had to admit that was pretty slick.

"Everything went crazy," he threw his hands up. "Max heard shouting. He looked up. Mr. Welles was crazy angry about something. Completely out of control. It happened so fast, Max barely had time to react. It was a blur. Welles pulled a gun out of his desk, he pointed it at Jonathan, and Max just reacted. He drew his own weapon and fired. He struck Mr. Welles several times in the torso, killing him. Later on, Max would try to reconstruct what happened for the police. Did he get some of the details wrong? Probably. It was a stressful, terrifying event. He did his best to tell the police what happened, because he knew he hadn't done anything wrong. He wished he hadn't done it. But, ladies and gentlemen, he had no choice."

He paused and pressed steepled fingers to his lips, a sign of sincerity and concern. He shook his head. "He had no choice," he repeated.

Very dramatic, Brunelle thought. Hopefully too much so. The jurors, or some of them anyway, would hopefully see through the dramatics.

Brunelle also hoped the jurors hadn't overlooked the fact that Ryder skimmed over whether Welles had actually fired a shot, or where he was when he supposedly extracted his gun from his desk, and had failed to mention anything about the semi-auto/revolver switch. Failing to address those issues so early in the case would help them become set in the jurors' minds. Maybe. Hopefully.

"Everything after that was a panic-stricken blur," Ryder asserted. "They grabbed Mr. Welles's gun, but then sold it to some homeless man on the street, even while keeping Max's own gun. Was that smart? Well, not if you were trying to cover up a murder, but Max never thought he'd committed a murder. He knew he was just protecting his friend. And at the end of this trial you'll know that too. Max is not guilty of murder. Thank you."

Ryder's return to the defense table was much more of the peacocking march Brunelle had tried to avoid. Strunk shook his hand enthusiastically. And they were off.

"The State may call its first witness," Judge Holmsund invited.

Carlisle stood up. "The State calls Detective Larry Chen to the stand."

CHAPTER 18

There were a few possible ways to start the evidence in a murder trial. In an assault case, it made sense to start with the victim, for several reasons. The first was they usually had the most information. Another reason was that the case would hinge largely on how they testified. A particularly strong performance could be almost impossible for a defendant to overcome, whereas a weak performance was best gotten over with so the rest of the case could be about shoring whatever weakness may have been exposed during that initial testimony.

In a murder case, however, the victim couldn't testify. There was no person for the jury to meet, assess, and hopefully like. So, one common strategy was to replace the victim with a close family member who could stand in to introduce the dead person to the jurors. Show them a flattering photograph and offer a little background on what a great person they were.

Welles didn't have anyone like that. He wasn't married. He didn't have kids. He didn't even really have any friends, as far as Brunelle knew. To know him was to find him irritating at best. The people who knew him best were the prosecutors and cops who battled against him day in and day out. As a result, Chen was as good a choice to start the trial as any. A substitute for the family member, with the bonus of also being able to testify about the crime scene and what the defendant said.

Chen entered through the doors in the back of the courtroom and walked forward to be sworn in by Judge Holmsund.

"Do you swear or affirm that you will tell the truth, the whole truth, and nothing but the truth?"

"I do."

Chen lowered his right hand again and took his seat on the witness stand. Carlisle stepped into the well of the courtroom, toward the jury box so Chen could more easily turn to deliver his answers directly to the jury, just like he'd learned all those years ago as a rookie at the academy.

"Please state your name for the record," Carlisle began.

"Larry Chen," he told the jurors with a respectful nod.

"How are you employed, sir?"

"I'm a detective with the Seattle Police Department."

"How long have you been a detective with the Seattle Police Department?"

It was all about establishing Chen's credibility. He was an experienced, seasoned detective. He didn't have any axes to grind. He had a job to do. The same job he'd been doing for two decades. The job that led him to stand over Welles's murdered body that night, and interrogate his murderer the next day. If someone as rock solid as Chen thought Strunk was guilty of murder, why should the jurors disagree?

When Chen had finished his recitation of experience, assignments, awards, and expertise, Carlisle moved to the night in question.

"Were you on duty the night William Harrison Welles was murdered?"

Chen nodded to the jurors. "I was."

"Did you know Mr. Welles?" Carlisle asked.

Chen nodded again. "I did."

"Professionally or personally?"

Chen thought for a moment. "Professionally to be sure. But in this line of business, dealing with the kinds of tragedy that we deal with constantly, you get to know people at a personal level too. You feel it the most with other officers, of course. The men and women who do the same job as you, who see the same things, fight the same fights, deal with the same losses. But you also gain a deeper understanding of everyone involved in the system. Prosecutors, judges, and even defense attorneys. I tangled professionally with Mr. Welles almost my entire law enforcement career. I think I got to know him pretty well over that time."

"And what did you think of him?" Carlisle asked.

Chen smiled slightly. "I'm under oath, right?"

That elicited the expected chuckles from the jury box. On top of everything else, Brunelle wanted the jurors to like Chen. If they trusted him and liked him, it would be nearly impossible for Ryder to undercut his conclusion about Welles's death.

"Yes, detective," Carlisle responded with a grin of her own. "You are under oath."

Chen turned to the jurors and told them the truth. "He was a thorn in my side. I never worked on a case with him where he didn't drive me nuts. He nitpicked every imagined mistake me and my team supposedly made. He came at us like we were the criminals instead of his clients. He was smart, prepared, dramatic, and ruthless. I hated getting cross-examined by him and when he was on the case, I made sure to double check that every 'i' was dotted and every 't' was crossed. And he'd still find a 'j' I forgot to dot. That was the kind of lawyer he was. He did his job as well as I hope I do my job. Professionally, I hated him. But personally, I admired him."

Brunelle smiled. That was exactly what he wanted the jury to hear. But there was a bit more that Carlisle needed to draw out before they got into the nuts and bolts, and casings, of the crime scene.

"In your experience with Mr. Welles," Carlisle posed the question Brunelle had made sure she knew to pose, "did you ever see him lose his temper?"

"Objection!" Ryder jumped to his feet.

Nothing said 'Ouch!' like screaming 'Objection' in a crowded courtroom. They didn't even need Chen to answer the question. Ryder had telegraphed to the jury what the answer would be.

"Counsel is attempting," Ryder complained, "to elicit reputation testimony in order to show action in conformity therewith, contrary to Evidence Rules 404 and 405."

"I'm actually trying to show non-action in conformity therewith," Carlisle defended to the judge.

Holmsund was not amused. "Either way, the objection is sustained. Ask your next question, Ms. Carlisle."

"Yes, Your Honor." She was more than willing to move on. Again, the jury knew what answer the defense didn't want them to hear. 'No, William Harrison Welles did not lose his temper.'

"Let's talk about the crime scene," Carlisle labeled the transition.

She took him through Welles's office, as if the jury were

with him as he did his initial walk-through of the crime scene. Carlisle punctuated the question-and-answer with photographs, each properly marked, identified, authenticated, admitted and published to the jury by projecting it from her laptop to the screen on the opposite wall of the courtroom from the jury box.

A wide angle of the entire office.

That ridiculously large desk.

Welles, face up and very dead.

Several more of Welles, to establish exactly where the body was, especially in relation to that desk and the wall behind it. Certainly not to inflame the passion of the jury.

The three bullet holes in the wall behind the desk.

The wall opposite the desk with exactly zero bullet holes.

The four—and only four—casings on the floor where Strunk was standing when he opened fire.

One more of Welles being put in a body bag for his transport to the morgue.

Carlisle took her time. They wanted to let the jury spend as much time as possible in that office, hovering near a dead body, the smell of gunpowder and blood in the air. It should feel horrible. And it should spark the urge to hold whoever did it responsible.

"Did you have any suspects immediately?" Carlisle asked, pulling the examination to the next logical topic.

"Not immediately, no," Chen admitted. "We spoke with the cleaning staff who was in the building that night, but they had been on a different floor and didn't see anything."

"So what did you do?"

"We pulled the surveillance video from the lobby."

So, Carlisle pulled that footage up next and played it for the jury, while Chen explained what they were seeing. First was the footage of Strunk and Beckle arriving. Welles walking to the front door, opening the door, handshakes and smiles all around, and disappearing again toward the elevators, Welles's amiable hand on Beckle's back. Time stamp: 11:16.

Then the second video. No Welles; he was dead upstairs. Beckle and Strunk sprinting through the lobby from the elevators to the exit. Nothing apparently in their hands. Time stamp: 11:32.

"Were you able to identify them from this video alone?" Carlisle asked. "Those are pretty good shots of their faces, aren't they?"

"They are," Chen agreed, "but seeing someone's face isn't enough to identify them unless you already know who they are. If I saw you or my wife on surveillance video, I would recognize you. But I didn't know either Mr. Strunk or Mr. Beckle, so we needed something more."

"Did you get that something more?"

"We did." Chen explained. They had to wait until the next morning when the business across the street opened, but they were able to view the exterior security video and see the car those two men ran to at 11:32. It was too far away to see their faces clearly again, but they were able to zoom in and get the license plate number. They ran the plate and the car was registered to a Maximillian Strunk. They pulled up his driver's license and confirmed the photo matched one of the men on the video. They went to the address on the license and found both Strunk and the other man on the video, identified then as Jonathan Beckle. They had the suspects in custody within twelve hours of the murder.

"That's some good police work," Carlisle remarked.

"It's just police work," Chen demurred. "But we weren't done."

"What was left to do?" Carlisle asked.

"We needed to interview them," Chen answered.

Carlisle smiled slightly. "You mean interrogate them?"

Chen thought for a beat, then nodded. "Sure."

"Is there any special protocols you follow when interrogating multiple suspects?"

"Yes, we separate them," Chen explained, "and let them sit for a while, to wonder whether the other one might be selling them out."

"Did you do that here?"

"We did."

"Did it work?"

"Depends on what you mean by that," Chen answered. "Mr. Strunk spoke with us. Mr. Beckle did not."

Ryder suddenly reminded everyone he was in the courtroom too. "Objection, Your Honor! A defendant has a right to remain silent. That silence cannot be used against him. It's completely inappropriate to comment on Mr. Beckle's invocation of his right to remain silent."

Judge Holmsund looked to Carlisle. "Any response?"

Carlisle took a moment, then explained calmly, "Mr. Beckle isn't the defendant. A police officer can tell the jury that a witness refused to speak with him, and Mr. Beckle is just a witness." She glanced over at Ryder. "Unless Mr. Ryder has something he wants to tell us?"

The jury didn't know he represented both of them. It wasn't relevant to what happened in Welles's office that night. But it could become relevant to what was happening in Holmsund's courtroom right then. If Ryder wasn't careful.

"Mr. Ryder?" Holmsund invited.

Ryder raised his chin slightly. "I will withdraw my objection."

Too bad, Brunelle thought. But if things went the way he wanted, there would be plenty of time for Chen to be able to tell the next jury that Beckle lawyered up.

"Okay, let's go through what Mr. Strunk told you," Carlisle began. It would have been nice to just ask, 'What did he say?' but that was too open-ended of a question. It called for a lengthy narrative response that hindered timely objections from opposing counsel. It also could be boring for the jury. The witness might forget something in all that narrative. But most importantly, that kind of open-ended question failed to take advantage of the focus an attorney's questioning could bring to specific parts of the defendant's statement. Carlisle took Chen through the interrogation twice. First, the things they wanted the jury to believe. Then, the things they wanted the jury to think were self-serving lies designed to get away with murder.

Strunk confirmed he went there with Beckle. Beckle wanted to talk with Welles about something. He was just there for moral support. He brought a gun. It was loaded. It was concealed. They parked out front. Welles came down to let them into the building. They went up to his office. It was a nice office, a big office. He sat in a chair by a table on the other side of the office. He wasn't really paying attention. Then there was a commotion. He looked up. He pulled out his gun and shot Welles four times in the chest.

Carlisle pulled up the audio of the interview and played that last part so the jury could hear Strunk say it in his own words.

They say to shoot twice center mass, right? Strunk's voice came over the speakers. *So I did that, but twice.*

Then it was time to go through the things they didn't believe. The lies that didn't match the physical evidence. The ones that were efforts to absolve him of responsibility for killing a man.

Chen: So we should have found five shell casings in the office?

Strunk: I said I shot four times.

Chen: And you said Welles shot one time. You also said he had a semi-auto, so it would have ejected a casing too. Your four shots, plus his one, equals five casings.

Strunk: It was a revolver! He had a revolver. So, no casings.

Chen: We didn't find a revolver in his office, Max. We didn't find any guns in his office at all.

Strunk: Right, right. I know, I know. That's 'cause, um, we grabbed it. I grabbed it. I grabbed his gun. The revolver. On our way out. After I shot him, I grabbed the gun and we ran away. Uh, and then we got rid of the gun, man.

Chen: How did you get rid of it? Where is it now?

Strunk: Uh, we just, like, sold it to some dude on the street.

Chen: Some dude?

Strunk: Yeah, yeah. Just some dude.

Chen: We're executing a search warrant on your apartment, Max. Are we going to find the guns there?

Strunk: Um, we only sold the revolver.

Chen: The revolver? We're going to find your gun at your apartment, but you sold the victim's gun to some random guy on the street?

Strunk: Yeah. Yep.

Strunk: All of a sudden I heard shouting, so I looked over and that lawyer guy was coming right over the desk at Jonny. His face was bright red and he was screaming something I couldn't even understand.

Chen: What was Jonny doing?

Strunk: He was, like, backing up. Trying to get away from the dude.

Chen: What did you do?

Strunk: I pulled my earbuds out and ran over there. I was like, what's going on, but the lawyer dude had totally lost it, man. He was screaming at Jonny, calling him a fucking liar and a bunch of other shit.

Chen: What other shit? It might be important.

Strunk: I'm not sure, man. He called him a fucking liar. And, how dare you threaten me? You don't know who you're fucking with. And, oh yeah, then he said, I'll teach you to come to my office and say that to me. I definitely remember that one.

Chen: Why that one?

Strunk: 'Cause, um, that's when he pulled the gun out of his desk.

Chen: The gun?

Strunk: Yeah, a gun. Shiny little semi-auto thing. He pointed it Jonny and started screaming at us to get out. And then, um, he just pulled the trigger.

Chen: He pulled the trigger? Are you sure?

Strunk: Oh yeah, I'm totally sure. That's why I pulled out my gun and shot back. To protect Jonny.

"So, Mr. Strunk told you that Mr. Welles fired a shot from his firearm?" Carlisle repeated it again. "Is that what we just heard?"

"That's correct," Chen confirmed.

"And you asked him again to be sure. We all just heard that," Carlisle said. "Why did you do that?"

"Because it was important," Chen answered. "He said it himself. That was the only reason he shot Mr. Welles. Because Mr. Welles shot first."

Carlisle nodded and took a moment to look at the jurors. It wasn't always a good idea to break that fourth wall and remind the jurors that everyone knew they were there too. Being a juror was a very passive experience. Suddenly being seen could be jarring. But Carlisle wanted them to know she was watching them as they listened to what she asked next.

"Was there any evidence recovered, any evidence at all, that Mr. Welles ever fired a gun that night?"

Chen shook his head and turned to the jurors. "No. Absolutely none."

"What kind of evidence would there have been?" Carlisle followed up.

"There would have been an expended casing," Chen answered, "if the gun was a semi-automatic. But when I pointed that out, he changed his story, as you heard."

"What other evidence would there have been?" Carlisle continued.

"Well, the bullet itself, most obviously," Chen answered.

"Where would that be?"

"If he had actually fired a firearm?" Chen clarified.

"Yes," Carlisle confirmed.

"It would have come to rest somewhere," Chen told the jurors. "Like the four shots Mr. Strunk fired. Three of them went through and through and lodged in the wall behind Mr. Welles. The fourth lodged inside Mr. Welles's body. If Mr. Welles had actually fired a gun, then there would have been a bullet that lodged somewhere, either in the wall or in a person."

"Did you check the walls for any bullets or bullet strike?"

"We did," Chen answered. "In fact, we went back and looked again after Mr. Strunk gave us that story."

"Were there any bullets lodged in the wall?"

"No."

"And when you located and detained Mr. Strunk and Mr. Beckle," Carlisle asked, "had either of them suffered a gunshot wound?"

Chen shook his head. "No. We would have noticed that."

Carlisle nodded a few times, took a moment to confirm she had nothing else she wanted to ask just then, then looked up to the judge and announced, "No further questions."

She returned to her seat next to Brunelle and it was Ryder's turn. Brunelle wondered how he would approach his cross-examination. Some less experienced trial attorneys felt a need to 'start from the top' and go over everything again with the witness. It allowed for challenges here and there, but mostly just afforded the witness a chance to repeat everything they had said on direct exam. Especially if the witness was an experienced professional like Chen. More experienced attorneys would hone in on a few important areas, hit on those hard and fast and sit down. The jury might be expecting more, but sometimes the scarcity of the questioning could suggest confidence, and the few questions that were posed might carry outsized weight. Ryder was an experienced litigator, but not an experienced criminal defense attorney.

Ryder stood up and walked toward the witness stand. Brunelle expected him to get a little too close to Chen, inside his personal space just enough to throw off his comfort. It was the standard position when crossing a cop. Instead, Ryder took up a position about two steps back from there. A little too far, if he had asked Brunelle. But, of course, he hadn't.

"The only information you have about what happened inside that office that night is from my client, Mr. Strunk," Ryder began. "Isn't that correct, Detective Chen?"

"Not entirely, counsel," Chen replied to Ryder, then turned to the jurors to deliver the remainder of his answer. "Mr. Strunk was the only person who gave a verbal account of what happened inside, but there was plenty of physical evidence as well. Things like the bullet holes in the wall, the location of the furniture, even Mr. Welles's body itself. Where it was located, how it was positioned, the number and types of wounds. All of that is evidence and none of it came from Mr. Strunk."

Ryder frowned. "Allow me to rephrase the question to suit your sensibilities. Mr. Strunk was the only person who gave you a statement about what happened that night, correct?"

Chen took a moment, then agreed. "That's correct."

"And without that statement," Ryder continued, "you wouldn't have known what happened that night, correct?"

But Chen shook his head. "I think we would have had a pretty good idea. Mr. Strunk and his friend were seen entering the building with the victim. The victim was then shot dead in his office, and Mr. Strunk and his friend were seen fleeing the scene. From that, it's not hard to deduce that those two men were responsible for the death of Mr. Welles."

"But the details," Ryder insisted. "You wouldn't know the details."

"Like who actually pulled the trigger?" Chen asked.

"Yes, like that," Ryder agreed.

"I would agree with that," Chen allowed. "Mr. Strunk was the only one who provided evidence as to which of them pulled the trigger."

"And my client said he was the one who did that, didn't he?"

"He did." Chen nodded.

"Now, why would he do that," Ryder posed, "if he was

the only one who gave a statement and he could have said anything he wanted, and no one could have contradicted him?"

"Why did he say he shot and killed Mr. Welles?" Chen repeated to clarify the question.

"Yes."

"I suspect because it was true," Chen answered. "He's the one who shot and killed the victim."

"But he could have said Mr. Beckle did it, right?"

Chen shrugged. "I suppose so, but he didn't know what Mr. Beckle was saying. Maybe we were cutting a deal with his buddy right then in the other room. Maybe his buddy was selling him down the river. Instead of lying and saying he didn't do it, he admitted he did it but then lied about why."

Brunelle suppressed a grin. *Especially if the witness was an experienced professional like Chen.*

"It's not illegal to shoot someone if you're defending yourself or others, is it, Detective?" Ryder tried next.

Carlisle could have objected. A witness wasn't allowed to give a legal opinion. But again, experienced professional. She let him respond.

"It depends," Chen answered.

"On what?" Ryder pressed. "Surely you can shoot someone who you think just shot at your friend?"

Chen frowned. "Your client said Mr. Welles fired a shot but the physical evidence says otherwise."

"Well, maybe Mr. Strunk was mistaken," Ryder suggested. "Maybe he was confused. Maybe he thought Mr. Welles fired a shot, but he didn't really. It all happened very fast, didn't it, Detective?"

"I don't really know, counselor," Chen admitted. "Like you said, your client was the only one who gave us specific details of how the shooting went down. I know what he said about that and I know the physical evidence doesn't support that. I'll believe him when he says he pulled the trigger, because why would you admit to that if it wasn't true? As to the rest of it? Well," he turned to the jury box, "I'll let the jury decide."

Brunelle allowed a grin at that. If they didn't like him before, they had to like him after that vote of confidence in their ability and integrity. Ryder needed to sit down.

Apparently, he was experienced enough to know that. "No further questions, Your Honor," he declared, and returned to his seat.

Carlisle declined any redirect-examination. Ryder hadn't really done any damage. Chen had done his job. The jury knew who William Harrison Welles was, they knew he'd been shot to death, they knew Strunk pulled the trigger, and they knew he was lying about it. Or at least, Brunelle hoped they knew that last part. Ryder had succeeded in planting a doubt that maybe Strunk was just 'confused' because 'it all happened so fast'. But either way, there was nothing left to wring out of Chen.

They could move on to the next stage of their case.

CHAPTER 19

Chen had previewed that the physical evidence didn't match Strunk's story, but Brunelle and Carlisle still had to prove up the elements of the crime. Ryder could spend his entire opening statement admitting that Strunk murdered Welles in cold blood, but if the prosecution didn't actually bring forward the evidence to prove each element of the crime, the case would be dismissed no matter what the defense lawyer said.

That meant a parade of cops and experts. The experts were what really mattered, but they couldn't talk about any particular piece of evidence without a cop first testifying as to the collection, storage, and delivery of said item to said expert. Chain of custody. It didn't matter if the ballistics guy could say that Firearm X fired the bullet extracted from Welles's body if some cop hadn't identified Firearm X as the one removed from Strunk's apartment when the search warrant was executed.

The good news was that it took time to call that many witnesses and that got them that much closer to the ruling down in Grays Harbor County. They had spent a week picking a jury. They just needed to spend another week slow-walking half the

Seattle Police Department through Judge Holmsund's courtroom. Because they really needed confirmation of what was in those sealed files before they put their very last witness on the stand.

The second to last witness was Dr. Michael Donovan, the pathologist who conducted the autopsy of William Harrison Welles.

Donovan arrived for court in a jacket and tie, with a file under his arm and a grin on his face. *Of course,* Brunelle thought with a small shake of his head. Even during the trial, Donovan was going to come across as a smart-ass.

"Please state your name for the record," Brunelle began after Donovan was sworn in and seated on the witness stand.

"Michael Donovan." That answer didn't allow for much smart-assery.

"How are you employed, sir?"

"I am an assistant medical examiner with the King County Medical Examiner's Office." Donovan delivered his answers to the jury as well. The studies said jurors liked that. And doctors liked studies.

Brunelle went over the good doctor's background. Education, residency, experience, years with the King County M.E.'s Office. Current job assignment. "Do your duties as an assistant medical examiner at the King County Medical Examiner's Office include conducting autopsies?"

Donovan nodded. "They do."

"What exactly is an autopsy, doctor?" Brunelle asked. "And what is its purpose?"

Donovan nodded again and turned to the jurors. "The word 'autopsy' is Latin for 'see for yourself'. When I conduct an autopsy, I examine the body myself, carefully and methodically, to uncover physical evidence that will allow me to determine the cause and manner of death."

"What is the difference between cause of death and manner of death?" Brunelle asked. He knew the answer, of course, after so many years of trying homicide cases, but the jury didn't, and they were the ones who mattered.

"Cause of death is the particular mechanism that led to the person dying," Donovan told the jurors. "For example, if someone dies because they were stabbed in the heart, we would determine the cause of death to be what we call 'sharp force trauma'. If they died from a blow to the head from a large object, the cause of death would be 'blunt force trauma'. And so on."

"And what about manner of death?" Brunelle prompted.

"Manner of death," Donovan explained, "is one of four broad categories: natural causes, accident, suicide, and homicide. Any particular cause of death could fall into several of those categories. Consider blunt force trauma again. If the object was a steel girder at a construction site that came loose and swung into one of the workers, killing him, then the manner of death would be accident. But if the object was a club or large rock or something that one person smashed into the head of the deceased, well then that would be homicide."

"And if they did it to themselves, it would be suicide," Brunelle added.

"I suppose so," Donovan chuckled, "although I haven't seen too many people attempt suicide by bashing themselves in the head with something. It's not a very effective method, I wouldn't think."

"Point taken." Brunelle frowned. Then he moved on. "Did you conduct an autopsy on a subject named William Harrison Welles?"

"I did, yes," Donovan confirmed.

"Were you able to determine a cause and manner of death from that autopsy?"

"I was.

"What was the cause of death for Mr. Welles?" Brunelle asked.

Donovan turned to the jurors. "In some cases, it can be difficult to determine a cause of death. That was not the case in this autopsy. The cause of death for Mr. Welles was very clearly four gunshot wounds to his torso. Three of the shots passed all the way through his body, while the fourth bullet lodged in his spine. That bullet was extracted and turned over to the police. The paths of the bullets perforated several of Mr. Welles's vital internal organs, including his lung and liver, and he bled to death within minutes."

"What was the manner of death?" Pretty obvious, but Brunelle had to ask it. Or rather, Donovan had to say it.

"Well, again, with any given type of injury, there might be several manners of death possible," Donovan said. "With a gunshot wound, it might be difficult initially to determine whether it was an accident, like a hunting accident, or suicide, or homicide. Some people try to make homicides look like accidents or suicides, so you have to be careful. However, again, in this case, the determination of manner of death was evident. A person might shoot themselves once in the head or heart, but it really isn't possible to shoot yourself four times in the torso, at least not without some extraordinarily advanced planning and a series of levers and strings. No, in this case it was very clear that the manner of death of William Harrison Welles was homicide."

Brunelle smiled slightly and exhaled. "Thank you, doctor. No further questions."

Brunelle sat down and Ryder stood up.

"Homicide," Ryder repeated. "But not murder. Correct, doctor?"

"Murder is a legal term," Donovan answered. "Homicide is medical. I'm only qualified to provide an opinion as to the medical manner of death. Whether it was murder or not is above my pay grade."

"Because sometimes it's okay to kill someone, right, doctor?"

Donovan pursed his lips and thought for a moment. "I would like to think that it's never okay to kill someone. But I realize that the law recognizes certain circumstances when it's not murder."

"Like in times of war," Ryder suggested.

"I would think so," Donovan answered, "if the deceased was an enemy soldier."

"Or when the State executes someone," Ryder continued. "That's homicide but not murder, right?"

Donovan nodded. "I doubt the State would ever define its own actions as murder."

"And self-defense," Ryder finally got to it. "It's not murder if you're just defending yourself or another person, right?"

Brunelle could have objected. Again, witnesses weren't supposed to give legal opinions. But the jury knew what the case was about. He wouldn't be gaining anything by trying to prevent Donovan from answering, except maybe making the jury think he was less than confident in his case.

"I'm sorry, counselor, but I really can't answer that question," Donovan said. "I'm not a lawyer. I'm a doctor. I'm a pathologist. I look at dead bodies and I tell you what happened.

I looked at the dead body of a man named William Welles, and I can tell you that somebody shot him four times in the chest. It wasn't suicide, and you don't shoot someone that many times in that location unless you're trying to kill them. Was that murder or self-defense? I don't know. And honestly, I don't really care. It's not my concern. And either way, Mr. Welles is dead."

That last bit came down nice and hard. Donovan was a joker in the examining room, but he'd been solid on the stand. He probably used humor to deflect some of the horror of his job, but when Ryder kept pushing, he pushed back.

Ryder took a moment, his mouth twisted in thought, as he obviously considered whether to push some more. After another moment, he decided against it. "No further questions."

Brunelle didn't have any redirect-examination, so they were ready for their second-to-last witness.

"Does the State have any further witnesses?" Judge Holmsund asked.

"Yes, Your Honor." Carlisle stood up. "The State calls Erica Mieneds to the stand."

Mieneds was the ballistics expert from the State Patrol Crime Laboratory. She was the one who would link the three bullets dug out of Welles's office wall, and the one dug out of his spine, with the gun found in Strunk's apartment.

She entered the courtroom and strode confidently to the front to be sworn in. She wore a blazer and slacks, with an open-necked shirt and short brown hair, with no makeup. She seemed very no nonsense, very capable.

Carlisle would do the examination. They had mostly been trading off, lest the jury draw adverse inferences from Brunelle not letting his female co-counsel share equally in the presentation of the case. Brunelle had done the previous witness, and he was definitely going to do the next one.

"Could you please state your name for the record?" Carlisle began, the same way they had each begun every single direct examination. She took Mieneds through the same preliminary information, establishing her as qualified to give an opinion as to the ballistics match between the bullets that killed Welles and the gun owned by Strunk.

Mieneds had a B.A. in mechanical engineering from Washington State University and an M.A. in the same subject from the University of Washington. She had gotten hired by the Crime Lab right out of graduate school and immediately began working in their toolmark division.

"A toolmark," she explained to the jurors, "is an impression left behind whenever a harder object comes into contact with a softer object. Examination of toolmarks has several different applications, but the one we see the most at the Crime Lab is with firearms and ballistics analysis."

"Why is that?" Carlisle prompted.

Again, an explanation to the jury box. "The barrel of a firearm is harder than the bullet that travels down it when the weapon is fired."

"Does the bullet touch the sides of the barrel when it's fired?" Carlisle asked as if she didn't already know the answer to the question.

"Yes," Mieneds confirmed, to probably no one's surprise. "In fact it needs to be in contact in order for it to receive the spin it needs to fly straight. When a firearm is made, part of the process is rifling the barrel. The interior of the barrel consists of a series of what we call 'lands' and 'grooves'. The lands touch the bullet, and the grooves are carved a bit deeper so they don't touch the bullet. The lands sort of grab ahold of the bullet, and they are twisted inside the barrel, so when the bullet is fired, it is hugged and twisted by the twisting of the lands. That way, when the bullet exits the barrel it has a spin on it that allows it to cut through the air and fly in a straight line. Kind of like how a quarterback throws a football."

"I see," Carlisle accepted the explanation. "And these lands leave toolmarks on the bullet, then?"

"Correct," Mieneds answered. "When a barrel is bored out, by an even harder piece of metal by the way, it leaves tiny imperfections behind on the surface of the metal. It's not perfectly smooth. It would be too difficult to buff the barrel down to perfect smoothness, and anyway, you wouldn't really want that because you want the lands to grab onto the bullet. These imperfections on the lands, just tiny little bumps, they scratch the bullet as it passes down the barrel of the gun. And since the barrel is harder than the bullet, those imperfections don't go away when a bullet passes by. And that's how we're able to identify whether a particular bullet was fired from a particular firearm."

Carlisle raised a hand. "Whoa. Let's back up a bit. How exactly can we tell that a particular bullet was fired by a particular firearm?"

Mieneds smiled and laughed a bit at herself. "Sorry, I get ahead of myself sometimes. I really like my work," she told the jurors. "Okay, so, deep breath, here goes. When a bullet is fired, there is an explosion of gunpowder and gas behind it that pushes it down the barrel of the firearm. Inside the barrel the lands grab ahold of the bullet and spin it. Those lands have small bumps on them that scratch the bullet on its way out of the barrel. Those bumps aren't planned'; they're just a byproduct of the production process. Those bumps also don't go away after a bullet is fired, so the next bullet will be scratched by the exact same bumps, in the exact same pattern. And so on and so on for every single bullet ever fired by that firearm."

"So, you can compare a bullet from a crime scene with a bullet you know was fired from a particular gun," Carlisle summarized, "and see if the scratch pattern is the same?"

"Yes, exactly," Mieneds confirmed.

"Did you do that in this case?"

"Yes, I did," Mieneds seemed proud to report.

"What evidence did you compare?" Carlisle asked.

"There were four unknown bullets," Mieneds answered. "Three were identified as having been removed from a wall at the crime scene. The fourth was removed at autopsy. That fourth bullet was extremely deformed so I couldn't do a full comparison."

"What did you compare these unknown bullets with?" Carlisle asked. "Did you have a firearm you were trying to confirm or exclude as the one that fired the bullets?"

"Right," Mieneds agreed. "I was also provided with a firearm collected during a search of the defendant's residence. I fired several bullets from that gun into a special chamber that collects and preserves fired bullets, then compared the scratch marks on the unknown bullets with the ones from the known firearm."

"And what were your conclusions?" Carlisle prompted.

"The three bullets identified as being removed from the wall definitely matched," Mieneds answered. "The fourth bullet was too deformed to compare all of the scratch marks, but the ones I could see were consistent with the firearm as well."

"So that firearm fired all four of those bullets," Carlisle put a fine point on it.

"Yes," Mieneds confirmed. "That's my conclusion."

"Thank you," Carlisle said. "No further questions."

She returned to her seat and Ryder stood up, but didn't step out from behind the defense table.

"Any cross-examination, Mr. Ryder?" Judge Holmsund asked.

Ryder rubbed his chin. "I don't think so, Your Honor. My client has never denied firing the shots that killed Mr. Welles. He was simply lawfully justified to do so."

Brunelle frowned at the gratuitous argument thrown into what should have been a simple, 'No, Your Honor.' But he couldn't totally blame Ryder. Mieneds's conclusions were hardly contested. But she had served her purposes. First, they did have to connect up all the evidence no matter what snide remark Ryder might make at the conclusion of the testimony. The burden of proof was squarely and always on them. Secondly, they had successfully run out the clock on the day, and in turn the week.

"You are excused, Ms. Mieneds," Judge Holmsund advised the witness. He looked to the prosecutors. "Any further witnesses, Mr. Brunelle?"

"Yes," Brunelle raised a finger, then pointed to the clock on the wall, "but it's already after four o'clock, Yor Honor. I don't believe we could finish the witness in the short time we have left, and I would prefer not to break up their testimony. I would ask the Court to adjourn the trial until first thing Monday morning."

Holmsund frowned. He had started the trial immediately after finishing his previous trial, and he would start another one as soon as the jury started deliberating on their verdict. The wheels of justice never slowed, and they were backed up. In addition to ensuring a fair trial and all those lofty ideals, the judges were also concerned with getting each trial done as soon as possible so they could get to the next one. Brunelle knew that.

"This next witness will be our last witness, Your Honor," he assured the judge. "We will rest our case on Monday."

Holmsund relaxed visibly. He looked to Ryder. "Any objection to adjourning until Monday morning?"

Ryder stood up. "Mr. Strunk and I are ready to continue our defense against these unwarranted charges now, Your Honor, and we will be just as ready on Monday morning."

Brunelle wanted to roll his eyes, but not in front of the jury, so he managed to restrict himself to a small shake of the head.

"All right then," Holmsund agreed, "we will adjourn until Monday morning at nine a.m. Have your witness present fifteen minutes before then, Mr. Brunelle. If you aren't ready to call this witness at nine o'clock sharp, you will rest your case without calling them. Is that understood?"

Perfectly understood, Your Honor," Brunelle confirmed.

If only he could be so confident about actually getting the witness there. That was another reason he wanted the weekend to make arrangements. The last witness was also the last person who would want to help them: Jonathan Beckle.

CHAPTER 20

Just because the trial day was over didn't mean the workday was over. Brunelle and Carlisle went up to their offices to debrief and prepare for Monday. Except the thing they needed the most before Beckle took the stand—part of the reason he was last—they still didn't have.

"No word from Grays Harbor County at all?" Brunelle complained as they crossed the threshold of his office. "Do they understand we're out of time?"

Carlisle pointed at the phone. "Call them. See what the delay is."

Brunelle picked up the receiver then looked back at Carlisle. "Do you have a direct line to whoever you were talking to?"

Carlisle laughed. "It's a small office, Dave. Just call the main number and ask for Jeremy."

"Jeremy?"

"Jeremy," Carlisle confirmed.

Brunelle frowned slightly. He had never liked the name Jeremy.

"Hi! Could I speak with Jeremy, please?" he called out when the person on the other end of the line answered the phone at the Grays Harbor County Prosecutor's Office.

"Jeremy Arnold?" the woman asked.

Brunelle looked to Carlisle, who nodded. "Um, sure," he answered. "Yes."

"Please hold."

Brunelle covered the receiver with his hand. "I thought you said there was only one Jeremy."

Carlisle shrugged. "There was only one Jeremy I spoke with."

"Hello, this is Jeremy." The call had been patched through. "How can I help you?"

"Jeremy," Brunelle greeted his distant colleague. "This is David Brunelle. I'm a prosecutor up here with the King County Prosecutor's Office. I think you were working with my co-counsel, Gwen Carlisle. We're trying to get some records unsealed that we think might shed some light on a murder case we have up here."

"Oh yes, right, right," Jeremy answered. "Say 'Hi' to Gwen for me."

Brunelle covered the receiver again. "Jeremy says 'Hi'," he whispered.

Carlisle waved it away with a roll of her hand.

"Will do," Brunelle promised. "So, any chance you have those records unsealed yet? We really could use them."

"Ooh, no, sorry." Jeremey sucked his teeth. "Our judges take however long they take sometimes, you know?"

Brunelle didn't know. But he was learning. "We kind of need them soon, Jeremy."

"Where are you with your case up there?" Jeremy asked.

"Have you charged it yet?"

"We rest our case-in-chief first thing Monday morning," Brunelle explained.

"What? Your case-in-chief?" Jeremy gasped. "So, you're already done. Do you even need these anymore?"

"We very much need them, Jeremy," Brunelle insisted. "We have one witness left and we have a very strong suspicion that those records pertain to this witness and to the murder victim. It will show the connection between them, which will show the motive, which will show that it was a planned attack and not a self-defense killing like the defendant is claiming."

"Wow." Jeremy clicked his tongue. "So these are important, huh?"

"Very important, Jeremy," Brunelle assured. "Very important."

"Okay, let me put you on hold," Jeremy said suddenly.

"What? No! Wait." But it was too late.

"What happened?" Carlisle asked.

"I'm on hold," Brunelle explained.

"He put you on hold?"

"Yes."

"Rude," Carlisle remarked.

"I would agree," Brunelle replied.

Then Jeremy was back on the line. "Okay, I called the judge's chambers and spoke with the bailiff. The judge will unseal the records first thing Monday morning."

"You just called the judge?" Brunelle was a bit shocked by that level of familiarity.

"Yeah, we all know each other down here," Jeremy answered. "That's just how things have always got done around here."

Brunelle expected that was true. In fact, he was counting on it.

"Thanks, Jeremy," he said. "Can you call us as soon as you have the records? I'll give you Gwen's personal cell phone number."

"Don't give him my personal number!" Carlisle protested.

"Ooh, nice," Jeremy purred.

"She's gay, Jeremy," Brunelle advised.

"Oh," Jeremy's voice fell.

"Oh my God." Carlisle threw her hands up.

"Call us Monday, Jeremy," Brunelle repeated.

"Okay, I will," Jeremey agreed. "But what exactly are you expecting anyway? How will I know if it's what you want?"

"We're expecting," Brunelle told him, "six court orders to dismiss, vacate, expunge, and seal the criminal record of a juvenile defendant named Jonathan Beckle. Signed and submitted by attorney William Harrison Welles."

CHAPTER 21

The other reason Brunelle wanted an entire weekend to prepare for Beckle was the very real possibility that he had disappeared. After all, Strunk was his friend, and Strunk's lawyer was his lawyer. It was all too common for witnesses and even victims—especially victims—to skip town once the trial started. Those overworked judges weren't about to adjourn for days while a reluctant witness was located and coaxed into the courtroom. The smart play was for Beckle to be visiting some distant relative a few time zones away. But the overconfident move was to have him take the stand in defense of his friend. And Ryder sure seemed like the overconfident type.

Rounding up people and bringing them to court wasn't really a lawyer thing. It was more of a cop thing. A detective thing. A Detective Larry Chen thing. Chen's thing was laying hands on bad guys. Brunelle's thing was signing pieces of paper to give to Chen as the basis to lay hands on Beckle and bring him to court. Brunelle could only sign a subpoena, not an actual warrant to arrest Beckle. Chen could ask Beckle to come to court, tell him to do it even, but he couldn't force him. That would take a warrant from the judge, and Brunelle could only get that if Chen served the subpoena on Beckle and Beckle stated he still wouldn't come to court. That was possible, but again not the move Brunelle was anticipating. Brunelle had to rest his case on Monday, with or without Beckle. Then Ryder would put on the defense case, and Beckle was almost certainly going to be his first witness. The only real question was whether it would be Brunelle or Ryder asking Beckle questions first. But Brunelle really wanted it to be him. Ryder wouldn't ask about Grays Harbor County and his preexisting connection to William Harrison Welles.

Brunelle drafted the subpoena and drove over to Seattle P.D. to deliver it to Chen.

"The judge said to have him there at 8:45 Monday morning," Brunelle explained. "But don't bring him until 8:59. I don't want Ryder to have a chance to talk with him before he takes the stand."

Chen accepted the paper. "I'll do my best."

Brunelle was about to make a snide comment about doing better than that, but then remembered Chen's best was always good enough.

CHAPTER 22

Brunelle spent the weekend wondering. Wondering whether Chen would locate Beckle. Wondering what was in those records in Grays Harbor County. Wondering why Beckle and Strunk had gone to see Welles. Wondering why Strunk had shot Welles.

The worst part wasn't the wondering. It was knowing that if he was wondering, then so were the jurors. At least some of them. He might be able to convince them that Strunk was lying and not just 'confused', but Ryder could spin that as a scared young man trying to talk his way out of a really big situation. The jurors would understand that, especially if they didn't understand why they went to Welles's office in the first place.

He kept his phone ringer up and checked his email, but there wasn't anything to do except wait. Chen couldn't do the scoop and drop until Monday morning anyway. And Jeremy wouldn't be calling Gwen's personal cell phone until then either.

It was a beautiful weekend, filled with sunshine and seasonable temperatures. He spent all of it inside anyway. Sipping bourbon too early and going to bed too late. Eventually, though, Sunday night arrived, with the promise of Monday morning.

Brunelle took to his balcony again. There was something about being alone in the middle of the city. A paradox that seemed to mirror his chosen career. Fighting for a single instance of justice in a world overflowing with injustice. The lights of the city were indifferent to him. His job would have been so much easier if the rest of the justice system was indifferent to his efforts. Or at least ambivalent. But for every Brunelle there was a Ryder. Or a Welles.

Brunelle smiled slightly. Welles.

Welles had been one of the worst. Pompous, longwinded, self-important, overconfident, condescending, dismissive, self-righteous. And he'd been one of the best. Intelligent, articulate, knowledgeable, prepared, hard-working, dramatic, talented, dedicated, dangerous.

Brunelle recalled the cases they'd had against each other, the clients Welles had represented. Karpati. Ashford. Nguyen. Countless others. Every one of them guilty of something. Every one of them protected by that pompous, self-righteous, talented, dangerous lawyer.

He shook his head at the memories. Brunelle didn't drink every night, and he wasn't planning on it that night, but he went back inside and pulled the bottle of eighteen-year-old Scotch out of the back of his cupboard. He poured a few drops of the good stuff into a glass and went back out onto his balcony.

He raised his glass to the city lights. "Here's to you, Billy Welles."

CHAPTER 23

Brunelle got out of bed early. He hadn't really been sleeping anyway. He was able to take some extra time to get ready. An extra-long, extra-hot shower. A full breakfast, eaten at the table, not on his drive to work like usual. Two cups of coffee before he left the house. He was ahead of the traffic and found a parking spot close to the entrance. He was earlier to work than he had been in years. And Carlisle was still there first.

"About time you got here," she teased from her spot in his chair, her feet on his desk. "Ready to bring this one home?"

"Do we know if Chen found Beckle yet?" he asked.

"Nope," Carlisle answered with a broad smile.

"Do we know what's in those Grays Harbor records yet?"

"Nope." The smile persisted.

"Do we have any fucking idea why Beckle went there in the first place?"

"Not a fucking clue." Carlisle dropped her feet and slammed the desktop. "Now, let's go win this!"

Brunelle finally returned Carlisle's smile, although to a far less enthusiastic degree. "I like your confidence."

Carlisle shrugged. "Well, without those records unsealed or Beckle in the back of the courtroom ready to testify, what else do we have?"

"Nothing," Brunelle answered.

"No!" Carlisle waved his answer away. "We have a dead guy and a lying defendant. But most importantly, we have a cocksure defense attorney and a friendly judge."

"Did you really just say 'cocksure'?"

"I'm pretty sure I used it properly," Carlisle defended.

Brunelle shook his head. "I don't think that's a word that could ever be used properly."

"Like 'twat-waffle'?" Carlisle ventured.

"Wow, yes," Brunelle agreed with a nervous laugh. "Please don't use that word in your closing argument."

"Don't worry, Dave." Carlisle stepped forward and slapped Brunelle on the arm. "If this doesn't go as planned today, we might never get to a closing argument."

* * *

Two out of three wasn't bad. Except when it was.

Chen was there with Beckle at 8:58.

Holmsund took the bench at 8:59.

And there was no word from Jeremy.

Brunelle and Carlisle stood up for the judge's entrance.

"Anything from down south?" Brunelle whispered.

Carlisle checked her phone, again. "Nothing yet. It's on silent. When he calls, I'll step out and take it. Just stall until then.

"Are you ready to call your last witness, Mr. Brunelle?" Judge Holmsund asked after directing everyone to be seated. The jurors were still in the jury room, waiting to be escorted in by the bailiff once the judge confirmed they were ready to begin.

Brunelle had remained standing, expecting to be

addressing the judge first. "Yes, Your Honor. And I have a request regarding the witness."

Stalling. But also a legitimate request.

"A request?" Holmsund repeated. "What sort of request?"

"The State's next and last witness will be Jonathan Beckle," Brunelle explained. "I would ask permission to treat him as an adverse witness."

What they used to call a 'hostile witness', but times had become more enlightened, and less direct since then.

Holmsund raised an eyebrow. There was only one advantage to calling a witness and having him declared by the Court to be an adverse witness. In fact there was only one impact at all. "So you can lead the witness?" Holmsund understood. "Question him like a cross-examination instead of a direct?"

"Yes, Your Honor," Brunelle confirmed. "I don't believe it will be effective to ask him non-leading questions. He has already refused to speak with the police and me on two separate occasions."

"I must object to that," Ryder jumped in.

And more stalling. *Come on, Jeremy…*

"Mr. Beckle appropriately—and wisely, I might add—declined to speak to law enforcement when they were investigating him for murder. He had a constitutional right to do so and it is unbecoming of a government servant like Mr. Brunelle to intimate otherwise. As for the second occasion, I assume Mr. Brunelle is referring to the time Mr. Beckle agreed to speak with him about the incident but then Mr. Brunelle broke his word, and his ethics, and refused to let Mr. Beckle speak on behalf of his friend. Those are hardly reasons to allow Mr. Brunelle to now badger Mr. Beckle as if conducting a cross-examination of a star witness. If he wants that sort of drama, I'm afraid he'll have to wait until Mr. Strunk testifies."

Ryder was a smooth talker, but every now and again his inexperience with criminal cases shone through. No self-respecting criminal defense attorney would ever telegraph whether their client was going to testify until the absolute last moment of standing up and formally calling them to the stand. Now, Brunelle and Carlisle knew they would get that chance to cross Strunk. But it didn't make Brunelle want any less to do the same when questioning Beckle.

"I'm afraid I'm inclined to agree with Mr. Ryder," Judge Holmsund said. "Is there any specific reason to think Mr. Beckle will be adverse to you in this particular proceeding, Mr. Brunelle?"

"Well, there is the fact," Brunelle offered, "that Mr. Beckle is represented by my opposing counsel in this particular proceeding, Your Honor."

Holmsund's brow knitted together. "Excuse me?"

"Mr. Beckle is also represented by Mr. Ryder," Brunelle explained. "Mr. Ryder represents both of them. I don't know how more adverse a witness could be."

Holmsund looked over at Ryder. "Is that accurate, Mr. Ryder? Do you represent Mr. Beckle as well as Mr. Strunk?"

Ryder nodded, but with pride rather than contrition. "It is, Your Honor."

Holmsund's brow dropped further. "Do you think there might be a conflict of interest there, Mr. Ryder?"

"Not at all, Your Honor," Ryder answered. "Their interests are perfectly aligned."

Until they aren't, Brunelle thought.

Ryder continued, "I have advised both clients of the

potential conflict of interest and both have executed written waivers. I am comfortable with my representation of both men."

Holmsund surrendered a small chuckle. "Well, I would hope you are." He considered for a moment, then ruled on Brunelle's request. "Given that Mr. Beckle is represented by your literal opponent, Mr. Brunelle, I will grant your request to treat Mr. Beckle as an adverse witness. You may lead him during your questioning."

Brunelle was pleased. Ryder seemed disappointed but not surprised.

"Are we ready for the jury now?" Holmsund asked.

"May I have a moment to explain Your Honor's ruling to my client?" Ryder asked.

Holmsund raised an eyebrow. "Which one, counsel?"

Ryder forced a smile. "Ah, yes. Of course. Thank you, Your Honor. I meant Mr. Beckle. I should like to explain how Your Honor's ruling impacts his testimony."

"Any objection, Mr. Brunelle?" Holmsund asked.

Normally, Brunelle would object to the defense attorney having a secret conversation with a witness immediately before the witness's testimony, but he wanted a moment to speak with Chen anyway. "No objection, Your Honor."

Holmsund sighed. "Fine. Two minutes. Then we are bringing the jury in and proceeding with this trial."

Ryder stood up, patted Strunk reassuringly on the shoulder, then went to whisper in Beckle's ear at the back of the courtroom. Brunelle made his way to Chen, not too far away.

"You want me to stay until he actually sits down on the stand?" Chen asked.

Brunelle shook his head. "I want you to stay until the end of his testimony. If I get lucky, he'll say something that will let you arrest him again."

Chen smiled at that. "You're the boss."

"No," Brunelle demurred, "but I appreciate the sentiment."

"Enough, counsel!" Judge Holmsund called out to Brunelle and Ryder. "We are bringing out the jury now."

Brunelle gave Chen a final nod of mutual understanding and returned to his position next to Carlisle.

"Anything from Jeremy yet?" he whispered. "I can't stall any longer than that."

Carlisle frowned and shook her head, eyes glued to the phone lying face up on their counsel table. "Nothing."

Brunelle nodded. "Cool. Cool."

"What are you going to—?" Carlisle started to ask, but then her phone lit up. "Shit," she whispered. "This is him."

The bailiff had opened the door to the jury room and the jurors were starting to file into the jury box.

"Take it." Brunelle jabbed a thumb toward the exit. "Then get back in here and tell me what Welles did for Beckle all those years ago."

Carlisle nodded, grabbed her phone, and scurried toward the exit, drawing the curious eyes of pretty much everyone in the courtroom.

"Is everything all right, Mr. Brunelle?" Judge Holmsund asked.

"I'll find out soon enough, Your Honor," Brunelle answered. "The State is ready to call its next witness."

"Then please proceed," the judge instructed.

"The State calls Jonathan Beckle to the stand," Brunelle announced.

An appropriate murmur rippled through the jury box.

The jurors had heard a lot about this mysterious Beckle fellow, including the fact that he had refused to speak with the police. The truth was, Beckle could still refuse to discuss the case. Just because he hadn't been charged didn't mean he wasn't facing potential criminal liability. He could still plead the Fifth. But that would have required him to think he'd committed some criminal act. And that would have suggested that Strunk did too. So, Ryder was going to allow his one client, Beckle, to waive his right to remain silent because it benefitted his other client, Strunk.

Their interests were aligned. Until they weren't.

Beckle stood up from his seat in the back row and walked to the front of the courtroom. He was wearing a suit remarkably similar to the one Strunk had been wearing for most of the trial. Brunelle wondered whether Ryder had purchased both of them. Beckle stopped in front of the judge and raised his right hand.

"Do you swear or affirm to tell the truth, the whole truth, and nothing but the truth?" Holmsund asked, his own right hand raised.

"I do," Beckle confirmed.

Brunelle didn't believe it.

"You may take the witness stand," Holmsund instructed. Then, to Brunelle, "Whenever you're ready, counsel."

Brunelle glanced over his shoulder at the courtroom doors. Still no sign of Carlisle. He could start the beginning of his questioning and hope she made it back in before he got through the preliminary stuff. It wasn't stalling exactly, but it would take a few minutes.

"Please state your name for the record," Brunelle began. It would be the last open-ended question he posed to him.

"Jonathan Beckle," he answered.

"You are friends with the defendant, Maximillian Strunk,

correct?" Brunelle essentially stated.

Beckle nodded. "That's correct."

"You've known each other for a couple of years, correct?"

"Yes," Beckle agreed.

"And the two of you were together on the night of the incident at issue in this trial, isn't that right?"

Beckle frowned. "I'm not sure I understand what—"

"When William Harrison Welles was shot and killed," Brunelle said it plainly. "You two were together that night when it happened, correct?"

"Oh, right." Beckle nodded a bit nervously. "Um, yes, we were together when that happened."

"In fact," Brunelle continued, shooting another quick glance at the very not-opening doors to the hallway, "you were the one who asked Mr. Strunk to accompany you to meet with Mr. Welles, isn't that also true?"

Beckle took a moment to answer. They had moved quickly from 'What's your name?' to 'You were the mastermind behind this criminal murder plot, weren't you?' He shrugged slightly. "I suppose so."

"You suppose so?" Brunelle had taken up a neutral position in the well, but took a half step toward Beckle to rattle him a bit. He had wanted to wait until the first waffle from Beckle before becoming confrontational. It would appear fairer to the jurors. "Either you asked him to come with you or you didn't. And you asked him to come with you, didn't you?"

Beckle leaned back slightly, away from the man demanding answers from him. "Um, yes. Yes, I asked him to come with me."

"To meet William Harrison Welles, correct?"

"Yes."

"Mr. Welles was an attorney, correct?"

"Yes."

"A criminal defense attorney, correct?"

"I believe that's correct," Beckle hedged. "Although that wasn't exactly why I wanted to speak with him."

Brunelle took a moment. The obvious next question was, 'Why did you want to speak with him?' but he knew not to pose it, even though the jury was dying to know the answer. He knew not to pose it for three reasons.

First, it was an open-ended question and he didn't dare give Beckle an opportunity to soliloquize about his noble intentions in visiting an infamous criminal defense attorney at nearly midnight. Second, there was the trial lawyer's maxim that you never ask a question you don't already know the answer to. And third, Carlisle had finally reentered the courtroom.

Brunelle raised a hand to the judge. "If I might have just a moment, Your Honor."

Holmsund frowned down at him, but Brunelle didn't wait for approval. He met Carlisle at their counsel table and lowered his head to whisper with her.

"What did they say?" he asked.

"Every single one of them was a motion and order to completely erase any records of criminal convictions," Carlisle reported.

"I knew it," Brunelle replied.

"But none of them were for Beckle."

"What?" Brunelle couldn't believe it.

"Six orders to erase criminal history," Carlisle recited. "Six different defendants. None of them were Beckle."

"Shit." Brunelle grasped for straws. "Did he go by a different name or—?"

Carlisle shook her head. "No. Lady Blackwell knew him by Jonathan Beckle. Those records had nothing to do with him. It's a dead end."

"Mr. Brunelle?" Judge Holmsund interrupted. "Are you ready to proceed? Or have you finished your examination?"

Those were the options the judge was giving him. The mid-courtroom strategy huddle was over.

"I, uh, I'm ready to proceed, Your Honor," Brunelle lied.

Carlisle shrugged and mouthed 'Good luck' then sat down to watch the train wreck. Brunelle turned back around to pilot it.

Lead, lead, lead.

Never ask a question you don't already know the answer to.

He needed the reason Beckle and Strunk went there that night to be ill intentioned. Not completely nefarious necessarily, but bad. He needed the entire transaction to be something dirty that Beckle and Strunk had initiated. You couldn't start a fight then claim self-defense. Going to Welles's office with an intent to do him wrong was tantamount to starting a fight. If Welles reacted poorly, that was to be expected, and not grounds to react with deadly force.

Brunelle had started the trial with a recitation of the facts he expected to prove. He then moved to inferences, followed perhaps too quickly by innuendo.

All he had left was bluff.

"Before I ask you about why you went to see Mr. Welles that night," he told Beckle, "I'm going to ask you a few questions so you know that I already know every answer you're going to give here today. I already know everything about you and I know everything about what really happened that night and why."

Beckle shifted in his seat. It wasn't a question, but he

answered anyway. "Okay."

"Your parents died in a house fire when you were five years old, didn't they?"

That question surprised everyone in the courtroom. Ryder included.

"Objection, Your Honor!" the defense attorney called out. "Irrelevant."

Holmsund gazed down at Brunelle with narrowed eyes. "What's the relevance of that information, counselor?"

"I would ask the Court to indulge me, Your Honor," Brunelle pleaded. "I will link it up in a moment. You will see in a few moments that it is extremely relevant."

Holmsund frowned, but nodded. "I will overrule the objection. For now. You may continue, Mr. Brunelle, but tie this together quickly."

Brunelle agreed. He had little choice.

"Your parents died in a house fire when you were five," Brunelle repeated. "Correct?"

Beckle's expression dropped. Hardly a happy memory. "That's correct."

"And you went to live at an orphanage called the Hutchinson House in Aberdeen, Washington, correct?" Brunelle continued.

"That's correct," Beckle agreed. His brows started to knit together. He was clearly starting to wonder how Brunelle knew all that. Brunelle needed him to wonder what else he knew.

"You lived in a series of foster homes after that, correct?"

"Yes, that's correct."

"And the last foster family you lived with was Margaret and Richard Quinn, right here in Seattle, isn't that correct?"

Beckle's mouth fell open. "Yes. But that information is

supposed to be—"

"I'm going to object again, Your Honor," Ryder interrupted. "None of this has anything to do with Mr. Strunk or Mr. Welles. All Mr. Brunelle seems to be trying to do is embarrass the witness for having had an unfortunate childhood. I would have thought this beneath Mr. Brunelle, but it appears I would have been wrong."

"Mr. Brunelle?" Holmsund glared down at him.

"The next question will link this all up, Your Honor," Brunelle offered. "I promise."

Holmsund pointed a finger down at him. "It better."

Holmsund leaned back. Ryder sat down. Brunelle stepped forward. "William Harrison Welles went to live at that same orphanage as a child, didn't he?"

Beckle blinked at the question. But Ryder didn't object. He'd demanded it be linked to Welles. Brunelle had simply obliged.

"I, I'm not sure," Beckle stammered.

"And Mr. Welles made it a point to give back to Hutchinson House and the other children who went through there, didn't he?"

"I think that's right," Beckle conceded. "I'm not really sure."

"He helped you, too, didn't he, Mr. Beckle?"

Never ask a question you don't know the answer to. Unless you're completely out of other questions and have to go from bluff to a guess. A hope.

Beckle took several moments to answer. He swallowed hard and glanced around the courtroom. Brunelle thought he might be fighting back tears. "Yes. He helped me."

"He filed a motion in King County Superior Court and got

all of your criminal history erased, didn't he?"

A reasonable guess, supported by the evidence, but a guess, nonetheless. If Beckle's criminal history hadn't been erased in Grays Harbor County, the only other county Brunelle knew Beckle had lived in was King. Brunelle waited for Beckle's answer to either knock down Brunelle's house of cards, or lay the foundation for Beckle's jail cell.

"Yes," Beckle admitted.

"All for free, correct?"

Beckle nodded. "Correct. He did it all for free. For me. For all of the other kids who got in trouble after they left Hutchinson House. He helped all of us get a fresh start."

Having found the opening in Beckle's armor, Brunelle thrust his sword into it.

"He was a good man, wasn't he, Mr. Beckle?"

"He was."

"And you went there that night to take advantage of him, didn't you?"

"I, I just wanted," Beckel stammered. "He had gotten so rich."

"You wanted more," Brunelle said.

"He said he didn't give handouts," Beckle complained. "That he had done enough for me."

"But you had a backup plan, didn't you?" Brunelle pressed. "In case he didn't just open up his safe and hand you a bag of cash. It was a shakedown. That's why you needed Mr. Strunk with you. That's why Mr. Strunk brought a gun. To scare him. But William Harrison Welles didn't scare easily, did he?"

"I just wanted him to help me a little more," Beckle insisted. "Everything is so expensive here. I was barely making it on my salary. I wanted to get ahead."

"But Mr. Welles wouldn't play ball," Brunelle could guess the rest. "So you threatened him."

Beckle didn't answer. It was the same as an admission.

"And when that threat didn't work either," Brunelle pointed at the defense table, "Mr. Strunk pulled out his gun."

Beckle's eyes widened. "Max did it! Not me."

"Why?!" Brunelle demanded.

"I don't know!" Beckle insisted. " I, I can't defend what Max did."

"What?!" Strunk jumped to his feet. "You told me to shoot!"

"I didn't mean it!" Beckle shrieked back. "I just wanted him to think you would really do it!"

Ryder sprang to his feet and extended a hand at each of his clients. "I'm advising both of you to stop speaking at once."

Holmsund, who had maintained strict control of his courtroom throughout the trial, leaned back quietly to let the scene play out.

Chen reached for his handcuffs.

And Brunelle knew they had won.

"How was I supposed to know that?!" Strunk screamed. "You're the one who said we could blackmail him! You're the one who said you'd tell everyone he sexually assaulted you and that's what those court records were! You said he'd pay so his reputation wouldn't be ruined! You said we'd split the money! You said all that and then you said to shoot him!"

The courtroom fell silent.

Strunk put his hands over his face. "Why did you say that, Jonny? Why?" He fell into his chair again and began to sob. "Why did you make me shoot him?"

EPILOGUE

Chen: Thank you for taking the time to speak with us about the incident, Mr. Strunk. Is there anything else you'd like to add to your statement before we turn off the recorder?

Strunk: I, I don't think so.

Edwards: He's gonna get a deal, right, Dave? I don't let my clients confess unless they're getting a deal. You need him to convict Beckle.

Brunelle: We talked about this, Jess. Murder two. Felony murder. They went there to commit the felony of extortion and somebody was killed. Classic felony murder two and about half the sentence he was looking at for the original murder one charge.

Edwards: Do better than that, Dave. I can get that from the jury.

Brunelle: If you really thought that, then that's what you would do. This is fair. This is justice.

Edwards: Justice. Ha. Do you remember that case you and I had with Welles? That psycho who thought he was a vampire?

Brunelle: Don't, Jess.

Edwards: Do you remember what I told you then? What you do isn't justice. You can't bring people back from the dead. All you can do is put someone else in a cage. All you do is inflict more violence on more people. You just pass the injustice down the line.

Brunelle: That was a different case, Jess.

Edwards: It's still true. You know it's true.

Brunelle: Jess, stop. It's okay. We all miss him. He was a bastard, but we all miss him.

Edwards: It's not justice, Dave.

Brunelle: I know, Jess.

Edwards: There is no such thing as justice.

Brunelle: Turn it off, Larry. We're done.

END

THE DAVID BRUNELLE LEGAL THRILLERS
Presumption of Innocence
Tribal Court
By Reason of Insanity
A Prosecutor for the Defense
Substantial Risk
Corpus Delicti
Accomplice Liability
A Lack of Motive
Missing Witness
Diminished Capacity
Devil's Plea Bargain
Homicide in Berlin
Premeditated Intent
Alibi Defense
Defense of Others
Necessity

THE TALON WINTER LEGAL THRILLERS
Winter's Law
Winter's Chance
Winter's Reason
Winter's Justice
Winter's Duty
Winter's Passion

THE RAIN CITY LEGAL THRILLERS
Burden of Proof
Trial by Jury
The Survival Rule

ABOUT THE AUTHOR

Stephen Penner is an author, artist, and attorney from Seattle, Washington. He has written over 30 novels and specializes in courtroom thrillers known for their unexpected twists and candid portrayal of the justice system. He draws on his extensive experience as a criminal trial attorney to infuse his writing with realism and insight.

Stephen is the author of several top-rated legal thriller series. *The David Brunelle Legal Thrillers* feature Seattle homicide D.A. David Brunelle and a recurring cast of cops, defense attorneys, and forensic experts. *The Talon Winter Legal Thrillers* star tough-as-nails Tacoma criminal defense attorney Talon Winter. And *The Rain City Legal Thrillers* deliver the adventures of attorney Daniel Raine and his unlikely partner, real estate agent/private investigator Rebecca Sommers.

For more information, please visit *www.stephenpenner.com*.

Printed in Dunstable, United Kingdom

70725065R00117